# SECRET SANTA FACE-OFF
## COMETS HOLIDAY NOVELLA

VICTORIA DENAULT

*For my friend Lindsey H,*
*who gave me the plot bunny for this book when she told me she hates*
*cucumbers.*

# CHAPTER 1
# NOLAN

t was a brutal practice. The kind that makes me think I'm too old for this even though I'm only thirty. Professional hockey has a way of making you feel like you're geriatric, especially when you're in a losing streak and the coaches push you hard to get out of it. Yeah, I'll be feeling the aches and pains from this practice well into the rest of the week. Thankfully, we only had two more games before winter break. I'm ready for a shower and a nap when I step into the locker room and my eyes grow three sizes bigger.

My teammate, and our current Captain, Xavier Oakes, is walking behind me and bumps right into me because he wasn't anticipating my abrupt stop. He looks up, his eyes taking in the newly decorated locker room, and he laughs—hard. I frown harder. "I thought we talked to management and told them we didn't want this crap anymore."

Viktor Volkov, our stellar goalie, cackles. "No bro, *you* told management we didn't want Christmas decorations in the locker room and dressing room this year. We didn't say shit because we aren't the Grinch."

I flip him off, but he smiles even brighter and pushes past

me, his bulky gear almost slamming me into the door frame. Xavier follows, clapping me on the shoulder and giving me a somewhat sympathetic smile. I think. It's hard to tell with him. He's such a joker all the time. "You'll live, Duggan."

"But I won't enjoy it," I mumble and march over to the bench in front of my locker. I know I'm being a total brat about this, but this team has become ridiculous when it comes to Christmas. Like, certifiably nuts. And it's all because of one person.

"I really like it," Viktor goes on as we begin to undress in the dressing room, which is also decorated within an inch of its life with garland and tiny, multi-colored lights and a giant blow up Santa in the corner. "I mean most of us can't be with our families for the holidays because of the tight turnaround in the schedule, so this at least makes us feel festive."

"It makes me feel like I'm wearing an Under Armor made of porcupine quills," I shoot back in a growl that only makes Viktor's goofy grin grow.

"Aren't you going to get a Christmas tree at home now that you have someone to share the season with?" he asks and then cocks his head, making a sad face suddenly. "Are you going to deny your poor kitten his first Christmas?"

"Leave Max out of it," I warn, and my heart warms just a little bit at the thought of the tiny but fluffy charcoal grey puff ball with one eye. I hadn't meant to keep him. But when I found him shivering behind a dumpster in October, barely two pounds with a heinous eye infection, I couldn't just leave him there. The vet I took him to put me in contact with a shelter but they said they were beyond capacity and they'd only list him for adoption on their website if someone could foster him. Somehow that someone became me.

"You finally named him?" Xavier asks, stunned.

"It's not his name," I argue. "It's just something I call him by until someone adopts him and gives him a name. It's a place holder."

"Uh-huh," Xavier and Viktor exchange looks I don't understand but I don't like anyway.

Not wanting to continue this conversation any further, I just glare at them and head to the showers. When I'm done, almost everyone on the team has fucked off, so I'm left to dress in peace. I throw on my jeans, boots, and Vancouver Comets hoodie and stomp my way to the admin offices.

Oh my God, I thought it looked like Father Christmas had thrown up in our dressing room, and our locker room that had a fully decorated Christmas tree with lights, fake snow and a million glittery ornaments, but now I know I was wrong. Father Christmas had only sneezed in the team's space. He puked all over this floor. From the second I get off the elevator, there's so many sparkly things and lights everywhere that I have to squint. There's also mistletoe above every office door and a five-foot blow-up Santa, complete with reindeers, in the conference room..

Felicity Roark's door is open, and before I even reach it, I can hear Bing Crosby crooning out "White Christmas." My eyes roll so hard in my head I think I sprain them. I lift my hand to rap on her door but she speaks before I can. "Nolan Duggan, to what do I owe this pleasure?"

Her smile is bright. It's always so damn bright but especially at Christmas. "I don't like the Christmas crap in the downstairs."

"Would you like some Hanukah items added?" She blinks those big, happy blue eyes.

"No."

"Kwanzaa?" She asks.

"I don't want anything added. I want it taken away," I bark.

She doesn't look the least bit surprised, and I realize she

was being sarcastic. She got the memo when I complained last year. But she doesn't care. She stands up, and I try to keep the scowl on my face. The fact is, Felicity is the stuff I fantasize about, physically. She's tall, curvy, with long brown hair she usually wears up and eyes that remind of me of cornflowers my mom used to plant in the garden for the very short time we got summer in Alaska.

"Your complaint was reviewed and we deemed it ridiculous. So the decorations went up," Felicity explains. "I did however, rein it in a little. I didn't put mistletoe outside the locker room door or put the inflatable reindeer in the tunnel to the ice like I'd originally intended. You're welcome. And if you really hate decorations, I would steer clear of the arena concourse until about January second. It's filled with all sorts of holiday décor."

The deeper my scowl gets, the bigger her grin gets. This woman...she was put here just to fuck with me, I swear. "Listen, Felicity I don't want to make a big deal about this but I will. I find it offensive."

"It's non-denominational," She explains. "All the decorations are Santas and reindeer, not Jesus and Mary or anything."

"I'm still offended."

"I can add more snowflakes to the decor if that will make you feel more at home," Felicity shoots back. Her perfectly glossed lips moving from a smile to a smirk. "You're from Alaska, right? You must love snow."

She is more frustrating than a broken stick on a breakaway. "Look, I think we just really need to focus on hockey right now, Felicity. In case you haven't noticed, we're like second to last in the division. That hasn't happened since—"

"Ten years ago, the Comets finished dead last in the league," she finishes the sentence for me crossing her arms over her chest. She's wearing a blouse that's red and as shimmery as a Christmas ornament, and I know it's on purpose. I try to focus on the fact that it brings out the pink in her apple cheeks and not the Christmas aspect. "But then we got a high draft pick and were able to draft this really talented defensemen fifth overall and our luck changed. And it will again. After all, we still have that really talented defenseman, and he's only gotten better with age."

Me. She's talking about me.

She pats my shoulder. I grit my teeth. She's the only person I have ever met that can anger me with a compliment. "Thanks but this talented defenseman wants the decorations dusted."

She casually walks over to her desk. "You're welcome to go above my head."

I know that will do no good. She's a total goody-two-shoes rule follower. If she says she has approval, she does. So instead, I huff and say, "Why are you so into the holidays?"

"Why are you so out of them?" She counters my question with her own.

I open my mouth but nothing comes out. I don't know this woman, and I'm not about to share personal details with her. So instead, I turn and stomp my way back to the elevators, trying to come to terms with the fact that I'm going to have to endure another holiday season full of sparkle and joy and all that other crap. I swear she turns up her stupid Christmas music when I storm off because I hear it all the way down the hall.

# CHAPTER 2
# FELICITY

What is his deal? I have been trying to figure that out since I started working for the Comets and ended up in an elevator with him first thing in the morning on my first day. I was on my way to HR to fill out a mountain of paperwork. I was nervous but excited and feeling happy and blessed that this job fell into my lap after some pretty massive...well, let's just call them hiccups in my life. I stepped into the elevator, and every nerve ending in my body took notice of him. He was in gray sweats, low on his hips, and a tank top, with a towel around his neck, skin glistening as it wrapped tightly around muscle upon muscle.

I smiled at him and said. "Good morning!"

He looked confused, so I said it in French because some of the players were French and maybe he was one of them. Because of that fact I learned while researching hockey for my job interview, I brushed up on some basic phrases. But as soon as I said. "*Bon Matin*" he rolled his eyes. "I understood you the first time," he said, his annoyance clear. "Yeah. Hi."

And then the elevator doors pinged and he motioned for me to exit before him, which would have been chivalrous if he wasn't doing it with a frown on his face. He limped out after me, and I later found out he was heading up to HR to sign some paperwork to go on leave because he had a torn tendon in his knee that needed immediate surgery. So I gave him a pass that time, but he's never been anything but aloof at best to me. And this radioactive anger he has towards the holidays turns him into a Class-A jerk.

I'm explaining this all to Martine, who runs the team's social media. We work essentially hand-in-hand since all the events I organize need to be tweeted, recorded, posted and shared. She's the only other woman in this organization who is my age, so we've been thick as thieves since I started. Martine has been here a year longer than me. She is smiling as I rant, which I'm trying to ignore because it's kinda smug. "I'm not the jerk here. I sat down with HR when he voiced his concerns after I decorated last year, and they consulted with Mr. Isles. Mr. Isles, the owner of the team for crying out loud! And even he said Nolan's concerns weren't based on religious or moral reasons, so we should continue as always."

"So Isles has asked him what his beef is?" Martine questions, tucking a strand of her short, brown hair behind her ear. "Why can't he share that so we all have more sympathy for his grumpy, but rock hard, ass?"

I shrug. I wish I knew. Martine pauses a minute to do something on the laptop in front of her and she focuses on me again, and her smile returns. "You've been thinking about him all night haven't you? Since it happened yesterday?"

I nod. "I have to go down there and make them draw Secret Santa names today. You're filming it. He's going to be all emo, which everyone will notice if you post the video. Or worse, he'll complain out loud."

Martine chuckles, leaning back in her chair in the staff break room. "I can edit out his grumpy, but still sexy, ass.

Honestly though, the fans love how grumpy he is. The female fans think it's hot."

I scrunch up my nose. Martine laughs and shuts her laptop, standing up. "Did I ever tell you that the female fans use the hashtag 'masturbation material' when I put up the grumpy vids of him? Maybe you should try that. If he gets you worked up, let him work you down too."

My eyes grow so wide it almost hurts. "Are you insane?"

She starts toward the elevators, and I follow with my Santa hat filled with neatly printed names of players and staff. She turns to me after punching the button to call the elevator. "There's no rule against inter-office dating."

"That man hates me, and the feeling is mutual," I reply. The expression on Martine's face says she doesn't believe me, which is horrifying. But the elevator opens, and it's got the head of our PR and an assistant coach in it, so the conversation dies.

We all get off at the same place, the bottom level of the arena, ice level, and head to the locker room. The team had off-ice training today, which means watching videos and doing weights and meeting with the trainers, but it ended about twenty minutes ago. When we waltz in, I make sure to put on my brightest smile. "Thanks for waiting for us everyone. Happy holidays!"

I get a round of hellos and heys from everyone but Nolan Duggan. Ebenezer Scrooge is leaning against the back wall, arms crossed in front of his hulking chest, glaring at the Christmas tree, trying to melt it with his mind or something. "So you know the drill. This is our annual Secret Santa gift exchange. You pick a name and over the course of the next couple weeks, starting tomorrow until the night of our community Christmas party, you leave a token gift every now and then on the desk or in the locker of the person you pick. Three or four gifts, total, over a few weeks. Nothing too expensive. It's not money, it's the thought that counts. Be fun, be creative and enjoy the season of giving. Now, who wants to pick first?"

Nolan is still staring at the tree. Viktor happily raises his hand. I bounce over there, making sure there is extra pep in my step, and extend the hat toward him, taking a moment to give it a little shake so the names mix a little more and the sleigh bell on the end jingles. Nolan finally looks at me to glare. I grin.

He sniffs. "What is that smell?"

"My Christmas perfume," I explain. "I only wear it in December."

He stares. And then the tip of his tongue breeches his full lips and skirts along his bottom lip. Slowly. And my eyes are glued to the movement like a wolf tracking prey. Only I'm pretty sure the wolf doesn't get the same tingling feeling in their lace undies that I'm getting. I blink. He speaks. "Smells like... an Alaskan wood cabin was set on fire in the middle of a baking competition."

"It's called Christmas Spirit," I blurt out. "You won't like it because you don't have any."

Viktor snickers and I frown and shove the hat at him. "I didn't say I didn't like it." Nolan mutters half under his breath.

"Yeah. Because being told you smell like a house fire is a compliment." I snap and focus on Viktor as he pulls a name and unfolds the paper to read it.

I move on to the next person, moving counterclockwise from Viktor so that Nolan will be the last person to pick. I want him to have to suffer through this. Last year he picked his name fourth and stormed off before we were done. But as Martine pointed out, fans love him for some stupid reason. As I circle the room, getting upstairs staff and players to take a name, something happens. I can feel it. A shift in the energy in the room. I glance over my shoulder as the hair on the back of my neck stands up, and I can see Nolan staring at me. Only now he's not glaring. He's smiling. It's stunning — because if I take my brain out of it, the man is gorgeous — but the grin is also horrifying. Something is up, and I don't know what it is.

Coach Baker pulls a name and then our head of PR, then Martine, and I'm about to move on to our back-up goalie when I hear Nolan's voice way too close to the shell of my ear. "My turn."

Like him or not, Nolan Duggan whispering roughly in your ear, standing less than a foot from you with damp dark hair and smelling of soap from his recent shower makes your knees weak and your panties wet. It doesn't matter how illogical that is. I try to force air into my lungs as I turn to face him and shove the Santa hat out between us to give me some much needed space. He sticks his hand in slowly—too slowly—with the same smile on his face that I don't understand because I've never seen it before. He pulls out a name. A glimmer of something dark passes through those expressive hazel eyes but it disappears instead of sticking around, which isn't normal at all. Then he nods and wanders back to the wall he was pretending to hold up earlier. Well, at least he didn't stalk out like every other year.

*What is up with him?*

"Don't forget to draw one too," Martine advises me when I'm nearing the end of the line. I nod and dip my hand in, fishing around for a long minute because there's only a couple names left now in the depths of the hat. I take my name and tuck it into the back pocket on my black dress pants and finish with the task at hand. Once everyone has drawn a name, I turn to the group. "Win it for Santa tonight boys!"

I give a big, beauty pageant winning wave and leave. Martine stops the video she's recording on her phone and follows me. "I got Betty from accounting. Do you know where I can buy knitting supplies? It's her only hobby."

I give her the address of the only crafting store I know of in

Vancouver as we pause in front of the elevators. I punch the button.

"Who did you get?"

I pull the scrap of paper from my back pocket and unfold it. My heart sinks at the very first letter - N. Followed by O and L and A and N and..."Fuck a duck."

Martine reads over my shoulder and starts laughing so hard she's doubled over when we enter the elevator.

"Laugh all you want, but I'm going to use this as an opportunity to make Nolan Duggan change his mind," I declare as the doors slide shut. "He's going to love the holidays by the time I'm done."

"Uh-huh," Martine manages to blurt out through fits of laughter.

# CHAPTER 3
# NOLAN

"A thousand bucks."

Viktor's jaw drops so low, his chin completely disappears under his scarf. He shakes his head and lets out a soundless laugh that sends a cloud of white vapor into the air between us. "As much as I'm happy to take your money for any reason, you hate this woman. I don't want you doing anything that might really offend her."

"I'm not an asshole, Vik," I assure him. "I just want to troll her a little bit with some gag gifts. I swear nothing mean just funny. So take the grand and switch names with me."

"Who did you get again?" He tilts his head, thinking hard about it as the wind whips his light blond hair across his forehead.

"The Wall," I say referring to our rookie center Jeremiah Waller. "He's easy-peasy. Buy some saw raw meat and a keg of beer. Done."

Viktor smiles. "True. And I don't know Felicity as well as you do, so..."

"I don't know her at all," I argue.

"Really? Because you spend a hell of a lot of time looking at her," Viktor laughs and more vapor clouds the air between us. "You study her like she's video footage of our biggest opponent."

"I don't," I growl and dig my wallet out of my pocket and open it. I shove the two hundred and change I have there at him. "I'll get you the rest by tonight's game, now give me her name so I can get home and get a nap in."

He laughs and hands me the piece of paper with her name on it and takes the money and the piece of paper with The Wall's name on it. He jumps in his Escalade and I jump in my Mercedes, and we turn in opposite directions as we leave the arena. Viktor lives in the burbs — Burnaby — with his wife and two, soon to be three, kids. I'm in a penthouse overlooking the English Bay. The ultimate bachelor pad in a sleek, modern building that thankfully doesn't allow any outward facing decorations for any holidays.

As soon as I open the door to my place, I head straight to my iPad and start searching for ideas for the worst possible Christmas gifts ever. Max wanders in from the bedroom and meows. I pause long enough to scoop him up and nuzzle him. "Hey buddy. Take a seat and help me put my evil plan into action."

Max walks across my lap, jumps up on the back of my couch, and lies on the back next to my ear. He starts licking his paws, ignoring my request for help of course. "Yeah, you got nothing? Me too. Maybe this wasn't a great idea."

The plan slammed into my brain like one of The Wall's hundred mile an hour slap shots. Get Felicity's name and make her regret the day she came up with this dumb Secret Santa idea she brought to the team last year when she joined. And if she grew to hate the holidays too, bonus. I spend an hour of precious pre-game nap time scouring Amazon and Etsy, and I come up with nothing. Some of the gifts are too harsh and others too goofy. I want to irritate her without upsetting her. Annoy her without making her feel attacked. It's a precarious balance, and maybe I don't know enough about her to pull it off. So I lean back on the couch, put my feet up, close my eyes, and make a mental list of what I do know about Felicity Roark.

Number one: she's gorgeous. The thick brown hair, those round cheeks that are always slightly flushed, usually with ridiculous excitement over something that annoys me. But still, she's a stunner. And those eyes. I'd love to see them glassy after a good orgasm.

Number two: she's great at her job. The team's community involvement has almost doubled since Felicity took over. She skillfully organizes food drives and free practice sessions with players for low-income kids. The team is on regular monthly shifts at a local soup kitchen. And the Christmas toy drive and party, which I despise, do a lot of good for people in need.

Number three: the way she sucks on candy canes in December and it makes me hard. I hate to admit that but it's a biological fact I found out about the hard way last year at the Christmas party. It was mandatory for players to attend. Xavier dressed up as Santa and handed out presents to under privileged families that were invited. I hung out by the food trucks trying to temper my annoyance with Kobe sliders and truffle fries. She was right across from me and the candy bar. So I couldn't help but notice the way she sucked long and slow on it, the way she played with it against her lips while she got distracted by something on her phone. I'd had to abandon the last of my fries and do a lap around the arena to cool off.

Great. Now I'm hard again just remembering it. Luckily Max picks this moment to jump off the back of the couch and land on my gut. I let out an oof, which he ignores as he circles once and curls up on my chest by my right shoulder. I close my eyes and force myself to try and nap, but it doesn't really work. I'm tired and cranky as I head back to the rink.

Turns out that pays off because I channel all the bad energy into the game. I make some big checks and some important puck steals. I even manage to score one, which I haven't done in seven games. We win the game in an OT shootout, but hey, it's a win. One point is better than none. I'm feeling better about my game, and the team, until I walk into the locker room again and notice that inflatable reindeer she said she decided spare us in there. It's blocking half the narrow corridor to the showers.

The other guys laugh and make jokes about it and even pat in on their way to the showers. I look for a safety pin or something else I can stab it with, but I'm out of luck. I storm past it giving it a quick punch as I do. The Wall is behind me, and he laughs. "Dude, did you just sucker punch Rudolph? That's harsh, even for you."

"Whatever."

I'm on my way out when I run into Martine. She's finishing up a Tik Tok video with the team mascot. I turn to walk the other way and take the stairs up to the team parking, but she calls my name. Damn it. I turn and try to remember she's friends with the enemy, but she isn't the enemy. "Hey Martine. What's up?"

"I just wanted to say thanks for participating in the Secret Santa thing without making a scene this year," She says. "I got some great video of it, and you're even smiling. It's going up on Insta tomorrow."

"Cool."

"Are you going to go to the Christmas party?" She questions and she looks like she would bet against me showing up.

"It's mandatory again, so yeah," I reply gruffly and decide to hit the elevator button since I didn't escape her. She stands beside me waiting for it as well. "Please tell me she at least had the sense to book the truffle fries guy again."

"Felicity? Yeah she did," Martine replies as we both step into the elevator. "They were a big hit last year. I kept hearing they were sensational."

"They were. You should try 'em this year."

"Can't. Allergic," Martine looks as devastated by that news as I would be if it were me. Her big brown eyes grow sad. "I found out the hard way by tasting the most amazing truffle risotto in San Sebastian, Spain on vacation when I was sixteen. My parents had to spend the night in a Spanish hospital while I got treated for the angriest rash you've ever seen. And I couldn't feel my tongue for a week."

"I'm sorry," I say and she gives me a small smile with a shrug as the elevator chugs upward. I feel this stupid need to bond with her. "I can't eat cilantro. Tastes like soap to me. Not an allergy but a genetic thing, so I read. Sucks because I love Mexican food and a lot of places throw it in burritos and stuff."

"Food is so weird," Martine says, and she seems really weirded out that I'm having a normal conversation with her. I guess I really should work on my disposition. "Betty up in accounting can't touch peaches. She says the fuzziness makes her palms itch for hours and Felicity gags if she eats cucumbers. She's not allergic, but she says, to her, they feel like slime and taste like dirty socks. She avoids them like the plague. When we go to Jimmy's for lunch, you know the place around the corner, she orders the Greek salad with extra pepper and no cukes. They make it special for her."

I smile. Wide. And it seems to weird Martine out even more. She blinks, and I try to rein it in because I don't want to tip her off. The elevator doors open, and I motion for her to go first, and then I march through them with barely a wave over my shoulder. "Later Martine."

"Bye Nolan. Have a good night and congrats on the goal."

"Yeah. Thanks. Just need to do that a hundred more times," I grumble, but as soon as I push open the door and walk across the parking lot, I am smiling from ear to ear. Like a kid at Christmas. Because I've just thought of Felicity's first Secret Santa gift.

CHAPTER 4

# FELICITY

I'm late! I am never late, but today I am. It will be a first since I started working for the Comets. My heart is pounding as I run across the parking lot, which is icy. I know this, but I'm punctual. I'm organized. I'm hospitable and...now I'm on my ass.

Before I even realize what's happening, I've slipped and — boom. One hand raises into the air to save the contents of the shopping bag in my hand, which is breakable, and the other goes backward to help break my fall. Pain radiates up my arm as my palm connects with the slippery pavement, and I wince. I'm also going to have a doozy of a bruise on my left butt cheek too, I'm sure.

"Are you okay?" I hear a voice behind me. It's Jeremiah Waller. The rookie the size of one of those mountains that skirt Vancouver. He's rushing toward me and uses his big bulging biceps to scoop me up like I'm made of paper and get me back on my feet.

"Thank you," I say and stare up at him with a smile. "I'm late."

"Are you okay?" He repeats and his blue eyes move to my

wrist, which I am trying to make circles with, but it's too tender.

"Yeah. Just sore. With a side of wounded pride," I reply and he gives me the sweetest smile. Jeremiah is a wonderful guy. Looking at him, he seems like a goofy frat boy. All brawn and no brain. But much quieter and reserved than he looks or acts on the ice. On the ice, he's a beast, never afraid of anyone or anything, with fast hands, a vicious slap shot and the ability to check people from one blue line all the way to the next. He's also single. And not happily. He told Martine, in one of the videos that she did already, in preparation for Valentine's Day, that even though he's only twenty-one, he's ready for commitment. Martine swears he wasn't just saying that for effect. Unfortunately, even if I could wrap my head around dating someone nine years younger than me, the big problem with that is I'm not attracted to the sweet, good guys who rush to pick you up when you fall. I'm attracted to the Nolan Duggan types. Tough guys who have shells thicker than a tortoise that I never seem to be able to break. At least I never broke my ex-fiancé's before he left me.

"I think you should have a trainer look at that," Jeremiah says as he holds my elbow as we make our way to the doors of the Comet's arena together. "It might need an x-ray or something."

"I will if it doesn't feel better by the end of the day," I promise, and as soon as he opens the door for me, I rush inside and give him a quick wave good-bye and another, "Thanks!"

But he isn't having it. "Come on, it will just take a minute."

He gently hooks me by the elbow and pulls me over toward the elevators that head down to the players' area . I should argue but then again, I need to sneak this bottle of Crown Royal into Nolan's locker. It's his favorite whiskey, and the store by my house had a Christmas promotion on it where the bottle came with a small crystal tumbler etched with a snowflake. It was really pretty and festive without being 'in your face' Christmas, so I was hoping it would warm his cold heart. At least it wouldn't make him hate Christmas more, right?

I step into the elevator with Jeremiah and pull my phone out of my back pocket to message Martine and tell her I'm in the building. Jeremiah watches me, so I explain. "I'm late. I don't want management to think I'm slacking off."

He laughs. "You're the hardest worker in this building and everyone knows it."

I smile. "It's nice to be appreciated. Thank you."

"We all appreciate you, Felicity. Spoiler alert, even Duggan," he says as the elevator doors slide open and—surprise—Nolan is right there in front of me. Jeremiah grins. "Speak of the devil."

"I think you mean Grinch," I quip, and I swear I see a teeny smile pulling up the corners of Nolan's sexy mouth. He's got these really perfect lips with a perfect cupid's bow and a great dimple in his chin and...I need to stop thinking about him like that. I make a big point of giving him a wide berth in the hallway while I pass by like he's contagious or something. His smirk grows even bigger at that, so big and sexy I feel it in my panties. I hate the way my body betrays me around him. Ugh.

Jeremiah walks beside me. "See you soon, Duggan. I'm just taking Felicity to see the trainer."

"Is she okay?" Nolan asks, like he cares.

"Slipped on some ice. Landed on her wrist," Jeremiah explains.

"Well, can she move it?" He asks Jeremiah and I pivot to face him.

"She is right in front of you, and she says I'm fine thanks," I reply and turn to look up at Jeremiah. "I'll go see Phil. I'll keep you posted."

I pat his shoulder and try not to wince when my wrist aches

even harder, and then I head down the hall on my own. I hear Jeremiah say. "She's not your biggest fan."

And I smile.

Twenty minutes later, the team's head trainer, Phil, is wrapping my wrist in a tensor bandage and my day has gone from bad to worse. It's a harsh sprain. Argh. And now I'm on the verge of being late for a very important strategy meeting with my boss. "All done. Now you'll want to take the wrap off tonight and ice it. Then sleep with it wrapped again."

"Okay. Thanks!" I hop up from the chair I'm sitting on and scurry down the hall. The locker room is buzzing. Players moving in and out. It's an optional skate day, so not all of them are here, but there's enough that I won't be able to sneak in and hide the whiskey without being seen.

"Felicity!" Jeremiah's voice echoes down the hall, and I see him lumbering toward me in full gear. His eyes land on my wrist. "Uh-oh."

"Just a sprain," I say and then lower my voice. "But I need your help. Can you keep a secret?"

"I'm fort Knox," He promises. "I know stuff about each guy on the team their own mother's probably don't."

I laugh. "Like what?"

He smiles. "I can't tell you or else I wouldn't be Fort Knox would I?"

"Point taken." I glance down the hall in both directions. "I need you to take this shopping bag into the locker room and take the Secret Santa gift inside and stick it in Nolan's locker."

His eyes double in size. "You're Nolan's secret Santa?"

I nod and he does something unexpected. He bursts out laughing. In fact, he's laughing so hard he has to put his hand on the wall to keep himself from tipping over.

"Why is that so funny?"

"I'm sorry it's just..." Jeremiah pauses and regains his

composure. "He hates this whole thing and you love it and...I just...I can't believe you got the Grinch."

"Yeah, well, consider me Cindy-Lou Who," I reply defiantly. "I'm going to change his opinion of Christmas if it's the last thing I do."

I hand him the bag. Even though he's staring at me with nothing but doubt on his face, he nods. "Okay Felicity. Good luck!"

He takes the bag and lumbers off into the locker room. As I wait for the elevator, impatiently checking my phone and punching the button for a second time even though I know it's on its way down, Nolan Duggan emerges from the tunnel that leads to the ice. He pauses, balancing on his skates and stick and stares at me. I pretend I don't notice, but I always feel his eyes on me no matter what I'm doing.

"How's the wrist?"

"I'll live. Sorry to disappoint," I snark back.

"I don't want you dead, Felicity," he says. "What's the fun in that?"

And then he winks. He freaking *winks* at me. This man will be the death of me.

## CHAPTER 5
# FELICITY

I make it up to the conference room just in time to slide into a chair as the strategy meeting commences. The meeting lasts forty minutes, and I struggle to pay attention the whole time. My wrist is throbbing and I can't get smirking, winking Nolan out of my head. Martine actually has to kick me under the table at one point when my boss asks me a direct question. She wanted to know if I had a designated Santa yet to hand out gifts to the kids. I said I would lock it down by the end of the day. I should've done that this morning before the meeting, but my stupid wrist injury and Nolan threw me off.

I walk back to my desk with Martine. "What happened to your wrist? Are you okay?"

"Just a sprain," I mutter. "I'm fine."

I walk into my office and sit down at my desk. I leave the door open and can see Martine as she sits at her desk in her office across the hall. As I shuffle papers to find my To Do list for the day, I notice a gorgeous evergreen colored envelope on the corner of my desk. It's got a sprig of fresh holly taped to the corner and in very simple block print it says, *To Felicity. From SS.*

Secret Santa! My mood instantly swings upward. This is one of my favorite parts of the season. It's just fun to get a little pick-me-up gift from a stranger. My family and I don't really talk let alone celebrate Christmas anymore, so this is all I get, and I really love it. Last year my Secret Santa was an intern from social media who worked under Martine. She was super creative and made all the gifts herself. I got amazing essential oils and a cute crocheted pillow with the Comets mascot on it and a really nice beaded bracelet.

I'm smiling in excitement as I grab my letter opener and slice open the envelope. There's a lovely, thick card stock inside embossed in gold and it says Cuke-gratulations! You're a member! In big bold letters. On the backside is a lot of fine print and with every word I feel my smile shrink.

*You are now a member of the cucumber a month club! There are over 100 varieties of cucumbers in the world and this year you'll be trying 12 of them. Every month for a year we'll send you a bunch of cukes as well as two recipe cards for inspiration. It's Cuke-tastic! Enjoy!(Memberships are non-transferable and non-refundable.)*

"You have got to be kidding me!"

Martine's head snaps up from her computer, and she looks through the open office doors at me. "What's wrong?"

"My first gift," I wave the card in the air. "A one year membership to the Cucumber of the Month club."

Martine cocks her head, her brown bangs tumbling into her eyes. "Is that a euphemism? Because everyone knows, sex gifts get you sent to HR."

"I'd be happier if it was, but sadly no. It's actual cucumbers," I make a gagging sound.

Martine tries to stifle a giggle and fails so I glare. She lifts her hands. "I'm sorry! I'm sorry! I just can't believe that's an actual thing. Who joins a club for cucumbers? That's insane."

"And who orders this as a gift?" I ask, annoyed. "And for me? I hate them!"

"Well, whoever it is obviously doesn't know that," Martine replies. "It's not a common hatred or anything. I mean, if someone gave me something with truffles, I'd have to cut them some slack it's not like..."

Her voice trails off until there's nothing but silence and her eyes seem to lose focus. She's looking at me but not seeing me.

"What? What are you thinking?'

She blinks and her eyes refocus. "Or maybe it's someone who does know you hate them. Maybe it was on purpose."

"Who would purposely give me a shitty gift?" I whisper harshly. And as her eyes connect with mine, a picture of winking Nolan Duggan fills my head. "No. No freaking way. Nolan Grump-Ass Duggan is my Secret Santa?"

Martine nods. "Yesterday I shared an elevator with him, and he was abnormally chatty. It made me nervous, and I had verbal diarrhea and was rambling on about food allergies and I definitely mentioned you hated cucumber. With a passion."

She looks remorseful, but it's not her fault. She couldn't have known that hot asshole was pumping her for information to try and destroy my festive spirit. I think about how I made sure his first gift was something he'd really enjoy. Something that might make him smile. Argh! "Well, now I officially have something I hate more than cucumbers. It's Nolan."

"What are you going to do?" Martine asks, nervously.

"I'm going to fight fire with fire," I say and grab my phone off my desk and punch my bosses number. "So I've got a Santa locked down for the party. It's Nolan Duggan. Yeah. I know, I was shocked too, but he insisted. I'll be there every step of the way to make sure he is the jolliest Santa that ever Santa'd."

I hang up the phone and raise my eyes to see Martine

looking at me with her hands covering her open mouth. "Oh my God he's going to KILL you!"

"He can try," I shrug and open my laptop. "Now get over here and help me with phase two. Picking out the most useless, annoying gift I can find for him."

Martine drops her hands from her mouth and joins me in my office. I grin at her. "Nolan says he hates Christmas now. Well, I'm going to give him a real reason to hate it."

Martine looks at me with the weirdest grin. "You two are going to either kill each other or bang."

"Kill each other it is!" I declare and ignore my fluttering girl parts.

# CHAPTER 6

# NOLAN

I swirl the whiskey in the tumbler that came with it. The snowflake cut into the crystal catches the light in a really cool way. Yeah, I have to admit this is a cool gift. Whoever got me did a good job. I sip the whiskey and close my eyes to the soothing burn as it goes down my throat. I walk over to the couch where Max is waiting for me so we can watch Netflix together. My left hip aches. A lot. I've been ignoring it for about a month, but it's not going away. I'm nervous to tell our trainer the ache is getting worse. It means I'll have to get an MRI and then... it might mean I need time off.

Max watches me with his one, big, blue eye. I gingerly drop down next to him and give him a couple of scratches under his chin. He starts purring immediately. "Yeah. I got you buddy. If only you could make me purr after a hard day."

His blue eye blinks at me and I chuckle. "I don't mean it that way. No one loves a pervy cat, Max."

He closes his eye and goes back to purring. I think about the last time someone made me purr... *that way*. And it takes me a full minute to remember.

My phone rings and I lean forward, place my glass on the

coffee table, and pick it up. It's either that or stop petting Max, and I'd rather give up the booze than have Max stop purring.

The Moms is the name on my call display. "Hey Moms."

"Hi Nolan!" They sing in unison. And then Mom D adds. "Just calling to check in."

"Congrats on your win the other night!" Mom Z says, and I can hear the excitement in her voice. Mom Z was always the hockey fan. She's the one who bought me my first set of skates and convinced Mom D to let me go live in Minnesota when I was fifteen and needed to play for a better team than our home state of Alaska offered.

I call them Mom D and Mom Z because I'm too old to call them Mommy and Mama, which is how I used to differentiate them when I was growing up. But as a grown-ass man, "Mommy and Mama" aren't coming out of my mouth so Diane Duggan and Zola Arbuckle-Duggan are now Mom D and Mom Z. Uptight, bigoted politicians will tell you that there are a multitude of problems for children adopted by gay parents, but honestly, that's been my only hurdle. Well, that and other people's homophobia.

"So what are you up to, kitten?" Mom D wants to know because childhood monikers are not a problem for her. I had to ask — beg really — for her not to drop that kitten thing in front of the guys on the last parents road trip. "Did you eat dinner? Did it have vegetables? You know you can't just eat your greens in powder form in those milkshakes you love."

I smirk. "They're called protein shakes and don't worry. My dinner was a steak and a kale and spinach salad with a big, double-baked potato."

"Nice," Mom Z says appreciatively.

"And did you have someone nice to eat that meal with?" Mom D is literally Cupid's disciple.

"Yeah. Max, my squatter cat," I reply without missing a beat. "I even let him lick my plate. I'm easy like that."

"Nolan," Mom D chastises but I can hear them both chuckling. And then Mom D adds. "You should try sharing a meal with someone other than a cat you claim isn't yours."

And we're off. There isn't a phone call lately where Mom D isn't subtly and not so subtly telling me to find a girl. I frown and let out a disgruntled growl, which they know all too well because I developed the sound as a teen. Mom Z steps in as she usually does.

"I know that you're so busy during the hockey season," Mom Z says. "And this season is particularly...grueling."

"Yeah, it's a bitch," I tell them frankly. But I don't mention my hip issue because no need for them to worry, and they would. "I admit it's been a while since I had a girlfriend, but I'm not lonely. I have a lot of friends and this cat I'm trying to offload."

I run a hand over Max's fluffy head again. He's stopped purring and is basically dead asleep now, his head happily on my thigh. I try not to think about how much I will miss this if... when the agency finds him a real home. But Max deserves better than me. Someone who has the time to dedicate to him.

I had an on-and-off girlfriend for the first five years of my career. Cheryl was a great girl, but I was too focused on my job. She was annoyed, and we used to have huge fights. Eventually, one of our 'breaks' was unending. We just ghosted each other entirely. I don't want Max to be annoyed. Or for him to ghost me. Run out the door or something and find somewhere else to live because I'm on the road a lot and at practice and stuff. So I'll find him a better home before he can do that.

"I'm sure you have...ways to keep yourself fulfilled," Mom D says, crossing the line of appropriate mother-son conversations.

"I am not doing this with you guys. Ugh. Gross," I mutter. "But for the record, I don't even have time or energy for that right now."

Since Cheryl and I blew up, I've had a few dates, some amounted to second dates, a couple to thirds. All involved sex, but none were ever more than casual. Feeling like I have to justify myself further, I add, "I'm not complaining. I like my own company, and I know I get hyper-focused on work when the season is on, which makes me impossible. And I don't expect anyone to get that. Maybe one day when my career ends, I'll have time to focus on someone else."

Mom D sighs. "You might be happier if you have more in your life than the ice now, honey."

And Mom Z turns on me too, which is unexpected. "One day you're going to find someone who you can't help but think about as much as you think about hockey. That's when you'll know you've found the one."

"Okay then. I'll be sure to let you know when that happens." I try not to roll my eyes because I know they'll somehow hear that through the phone. "How's work?"

"Fine. Same."

"How's the guys you work with?" I ask more pointedly.

"Same," Mom D says flatly, like she's finally as tired of it all as I am for them. My moms run their own construction company in Gnome Alaska. It's a male-dominated industry, filled with a lot of macho dudes who don't know what to do with a married lesbian couple telling them what to do. Also, Mom Z inherited her parents' small fishing lodge and she manages that. It makes vacations and holidays hell. But they're both workaholics, so they're happy.

"You still planning a vacation in April?" I ask.

"We will be at the last game of your regular season, as always," Mom Z promises.

"Wouldn't miss it," Mom D confirms. "Give that cat of yours a kiss for us."

"I don't kiss Max," I wrinkle my nose at the thought. "And he's not *my* cat."

"Uh-huh…" they reply in unison and then, before I can argue further Mom Z adds, "Love you son. Talk soon."

And they hang up.

I drop my phone on the couch beside me and gingerly reach for my scotch again, trying not to disturb Max. After successfully obtaining the tumbler and taking a sip, my thoughts inexplicably drift to Felicity. She must have found her Secret Santa gift today. I wonder how annoyed it made her. I hope she got all flushed and bothered… I bet she looks incredible with some pink in her cheeks. I wonder if she flushes when she masturbates? And now I'm picturing her laid out on her bed, naked and dewy after a shower maybe. Her fingers sliding over her taut pale skin, to that perfect spot between her legs. And…

My phone rings again. Scaring both me and my boner. When I startle, Max jumps and scurries off the couch and directly under it. He's still a bit skittish from being abandoned and living on the streets. "I'm sorry buddy! It's okay. You can come out."

My phone continues to jingle beside me, and I glance at the screen. It's my manager, Todd Baylord. I have no idea why he'd be calling me at all, let alone so late on a weekday. If I didn't have a no trade clause, I'd be panicking a little. No one wants an unexpected late night call from an agent or manager when they play pro sports. Never a good sign.

"Todd?" I say as I accept the call. "Everything okay?"

"No," he says bluntly, which isn't at all like him. I sit straighter and brace myself. "I just got a call from Maureen."

"Maureen?" My brain scrambles to figure out who that is. It's vaguely familiar.

"Maureen Callahan. Your agent Rick's wife," Todd explains. "Rick had a heart attack. He's dead, Nolan."

"Oh shit," I gasp. Rick was older, sure but had seemed like he was in great shape. And he said his job kept him going. He never wanted to retire. And now he never will. "Oh my God, poor Maureen and the kids."

"Yeah. It's rough," Todd agrees. "And I wanted to let you know firsthand. So you didn't hear it in the news or anything."

"I'll call her in the next few days," I promise. "And be at the funeral if I can, of course. And send something."

"Yeah, I'll keep you posted on all that too. But Nolan," Todd says his voice changing, growing even more repentant as he adds. "This means you're agentless. You'll need to rectify that sooner rather than later. With your contract coming up at the end of the season and the struggle going on right now with the team... you need someone strong like Rick was. Someone who knows your worth and will fight for you."

"Yeah. I just... it's not the time to focus on that."

"Agreed. But I wouldn't be doing my job if I didn't at least mention it," Todd replies. "I'll keep you posted on funeral details. And condolences, Nolan. I know he was with you from the start."

"Yeah. Thanks. But let's focus on Maureen. They were together forty years. I can't even imagine that loss," I reply and then thank him again and end the call.

I drop my head back against the couch and put down my scotch, no longer interested in the booze. Rick Callahan was my agent from the time I was seventeen. He was kind and fatherly. Well, more like grandfatherly since he was already sixty when he signed me. But he was a constant. And he never steered me wrong. I feel this loss on a multitude of levels.

Max jumps back onto the couch and climbs right into my lap. He stares up at me blinking. Lets out one soft meow, like he's trying to offer me condolences too, and then curls up directly in the middle of my lap.

Well, tonight took a turn, and the world feels a little dimmer without Rick. I hate to admit it, but I think in this case, I wish my moms were right and I had someone to talk to about the heavy stuff like this. Someone who doesn't also wear skates for a living or manage the people who do.

I sigh and pet Max until he starts to purr again.

## CHAPTER 7
# FELICITY

"Oh! I adore this song!" I gush and take the garland I'm holding and dance around the tiny space that is my living room.

Ellery laughs at me from her position tucked into the corner of my L-shaped couch. She's got my Christmas throw blanket, forest green with sparkly off-white snowflakes on it, wrapped around her. She is begrudgingly still wearing the Santa hat I gave her when she walked in the door. Ellery doesn't hate Christmas, but I know she only volunteered to hang out and help me decorate my apartment because I said I'd make my infamous Cranberry spice martinis.

"Maybe Nolan is right and you are a rabid, little elf," Ellery laughs as Michael Bublé croons "Have a Holly Jolly Christmas" and I continue to dance.

"Do not mention that name tonight," I warn her and finally swing myself and the garland over to the curved entrance to the kitchen. I pull out a step ladder and climb up to hang the garland from the little hooks I've already placed there. "This is about getting my mind off him, remember?"

I glance over my shoulder and see Ellery's big brown eyes

land on the scarf. The garish yellow wool monstrosity he gave me as my last Secret Santa gift. Well, not last ever. As the rules go, I probably have one more horrible thing to endure before the big party, which signals the end of our gift exchange.

"Right. So we aren't allowed to talk about how you two have enough sexual chemistry to melt all the ice in the arena my dad owns," Ellery says frankly and then takes a slow sip from her martini as I glare so hard at her I almost fall off the step ladder.

I manage to right myself before tumbling and finish hanging the garland before jumping down and reaching for my own martini on the coffee table. If she's going to insist on talking Nolan Duggan, I definitely need a drink.

"He's torturing me," I mutter. "On purpose. And I'm retaliating. How is that hot?"

"Tell me you don't think he's sexy, even just a little bit," Ellery lifts a pale eyebrow and quirks her lip over her martini glass. "The grumbling, the brooding, the frowning. You don't think it's kinda like foreplay. The way he singles you out for his best worst attitude?"

"No." I say it firmly, but then I bite my lip. "I don't think it's foreplay but... I mean the man somehow makes it work. The grumpiness. Sometimes. Rarely but sometimes... it's mildly intoxicating."

Ellery woops so loud I can't hear Bublé for a second, so I immediately gulp down some of my tart martini creation and lick the spicy sugar from the rim off my lips before adding. "But I'm vulnerable to just about anything nowadays. I've been single far too long. I can find just about anything sexy at this point. It's called desperation."

"You are far from desperate. You've purposely avoided men like the plague and rightfully so," Ellery reaches over and squeezes my knee, which is covered in my favorite Christmas pajama bottoms. The ones with extra-long wiener dogs tangled up in Christmas lights all over them. "It's been what now? Two years? You definitely need to put yourself back out there."

"Two years on Christmas day. And yeah, maybe I do," I admit because what I haven't told anyone, not even my best friend Ellery, is I had a vibrant sex dream about Nolan the other night that had me panting when I woke up. I had to masturbate to the memory before it faded. I'm not proud, but I couldn't avoid it. It felt way too good. And I don't even like him. I can't imagine what fantasizing about someone I'd like would be like. Someone I could actually date without wanting to punch. I look at Ellery again instead of staring at my half-decorated Christmas tree. "But the thing is, I don't have time to date. I love my job and devote a lot of time at the office. The idea of giving up what little spare time I have to go on awkward first dates with randos I meet on the internet is not appealing."

"So date a hockey player," Ellery smiles.

"Do not say —"

"Nolan Duggan is single."

"You are evil." I declare and Ellery laughs manically. "You shouldn't encourage inter-office fraternization within your father's hockey franchise."

"Why the hell not?" Ellery demands and sips the last of her martini. "It's not against policy for a reason. My dad met my step-monster because she was head of marketing for his tech company remember?"

"And you call her step-monster, and the marriage lasted forty months, so what does that tell you?" I reply.

Ellery sighs. "The divorce proceedings lasted longer than the marriage, but all that really tells you is that my dad has terrible taste in women. Don't let that make you afraid to try."

"I have my own reasons to be afraid remember?" I mutter, and Ellery's gaze softens. She remembers just as well as I do, after all she was supposed to be my maid of honor but instead, she spent my wedding day handing me tissues and letting me literally cry on her shoulder.

I pluck her empty martini glass from her hands, down the rest of mine and get up off the couch. "Another?"

"Do you have to even ask?" Ellery replies.

"Alexa, play that song again," I call out, and Michael Bublé's "Holly Joly Christmas" starts over. Ellery groans, but I sing along as I make the martinis. Until my phone starts playing "Jingle Bells."

"Alexa pause!"

The music stops, and Ellery, who is peering at my phone on the coffee table in front of her, glances up at me with a furrowed brow. "It's your parents."

"Shit."

"Ignore it," Ellery suggests with a sympathetic smile.

I sigh and carry over her martini. After handing it to her, I reach for the phone. "I can't. They've already called twice today, and I've let it go to voicemail both times. I can't outrun them, unfortunately."

Ellery looks as annoyed as I feel. She gets along great with her dad but has never liked any of his wives, so she's sympathetic to my family drama. However, these are my actual biological parents, not a step-parent. They're happily married and totally in love... with my ex-fiancé. I drop down on the couch beside Ellery as she lowers the music, and I hit answer. I close my eyes and keep my tone light. "Hey!"

"Oh good. You answered, finally," my mother's voice fills my ear. "It's your mom."

"And your dad!" I hear Dad's cheerful baritone and realize I'm on speaker.

"I know. I have call display," I explain. "You would too if you got cellphones."

"Don't need those," Dad says. "I'd walk into traffic if I had one of those damn things. You know how easily I get distracted."

He does. Dad has ADHD and likes to do twelve things at once. A cellphone would make his head explode, but I still wish they had one for emergencies. Mom clears her throat. "Well we won't keep you. I suppose you've got a lot going on at that job what with the holidays almost here."

"Yeah. It's busy," I say and clench my jaw. She always sounds so eager to stop talking to me, even when she's the one who calls. "But I have a minute. How are you two? How's Gonzo?"

Gonzo is my parent's parrot. He hates me. Always has. When I was a teenager, he used to dive bomb me in the kitchen, where my parents often left his cage door open. I secretly hope he's dead every time I ask. Horrible I know, but in my defense, he's also how I found out that my fiancé was banging my cousin. On Christmas Eve. Less than a week before our wedding.

"He's good," Dad tells me. "We got him his Christmas presents already."

"Lucky boy," I mutter.

"We got you presents too, honey," Mom interjects. "That's why I'm calling. I was wondering if I should be mailing them to Vancouver or if you're coming back home this Christmas."

It's literally two weeks away and this is the first time they thought to ask? Really?

"I won't be home," I explain and then blame the team, which is not accurate. Yes, they have games on the twenty-third and the twenty-seventh but I could easily fly back to my home-town of Kelowna in that time. Hell, I could even drive. And back-end staff like me doesn't have to be here for every single game. After the Community Christmas Party in two days, I don't have another event to run until the first week of January. But I'd rather spend Christmas with grinchy Nolan Duggan than my family. "Work is crazy. And Ellery and her family have been kind enough to invite me to theirs for Christmas day, so don't worry about me."

"Oh. Okay," Dad at least sounds a wee bit disappointed. "We'll miss you. And we'll call you, of course."

"We could Facetime if you guys had cellphones. Or Facebook accounts," I reply.

Ellery sips her martini, eyes stuck to my face trying to read the situation since she can't hear their end of the conversation. Dad just chuckles at that. "I told you, I'm not giving in just yet."

"Maybe we could Zoom," Mom suggests. "I learned how to do that at work."

"Okay. Sure." I say.

"But since you're not coming home, I just wanted to tell you..." Mom pauses and I know that I'm going to hate whatever comes out of her mouth next. "We're going to go to Auntie Liz's for Christmas day this year."

"What?"

"Oh Felicity, we wouldn't do it if you were coming home, obviously," Mom says, sounding annoyed. Like I'm the problem here. "But you aren't. So why should Dad and I sit here by ourselves?"

"No. Yeah. Okay," I sputter. "Go spend it with Liz and her daughter and my ex-fiancé. That's reasonable."

"That's not reasonable," Ellery hisses and hands me her martini. I take a big ass gulp.

"Felicity are you still really upset about that?" Dad asks softly. "I mean, it's been years and you seem to be doing just fine. And he always asks about you, you know."

"No. I don't know, because I'm not the one working with

him," I bark out and instantly regret it. My father loves any chance to play the victim.

"I have a job Felicity. One that put you through college debt-free and keeps food on the table for your mother and I," he says flatly. "I can't sacrifice our well-being because you got your feelings hurt."

"My feelings hurt?" I spit out. "Bryce was my fiancé and he was sleeping with my cousin. I had to cancel my wedding and find a new job and move my entire life."

"You could have kept working in Seattle. He had nothing to do with your job," Mom reminds me. "He played on a different team."

"Yeah," I swallow and hate that after two years, there's still a lump in my throat when this comes up. But now it's not about Bryce. It's about my parents essentially picking him over me after it all went down.

"I'm not coming home from Christmas," I say after a shuddering breath and another gulp of Ellery's martini. "Go break bread with Aunt Liz, her whore of a daughter Jennifer and her boyfriend also known as my cheating ex. Merry Christmas!"

I punch end and toss my phone onto the chair across the room. It bounces on the seat cushion and stills. When it rings again, I ignore it. I know it's my parents calling me back. Ellery unwraps herself from the blanket and reaches over and hugs me. "I swear to God your dad is whacked," she says sympathetically. "He should have dropped Bryce as a client when he was caught cheating on you."

"I agree, but he clearly can separate family from being a sports agent," I mutter and fight against the tears threatening to spill from my eyes. "And he's not even a major league player yet. He may never be. He doesn't bring in a ton of money for my dad. He's a long shot. A shitty, cheating long shot who my stupid cousin Jennifer will likely marry."

"Can I be your plus one at that wedding?" Ellery whispers as she squeezes me again. "I promise to get drunk and be belligerent and puke on the wedding cake."

I bark out a laugh at that. As I pull away, she waves at the drink still in my hand, encouraging me to finish it. So I take another sip. She sighs. "You know if I told my dad one of his players did something as insignificant as not holding a door open for me at the arena, he'd offer to trade him. And your dad can't just drop this douche? So not cool."

I nod in agreement, and then I give her a weak but cheeky smile. "If you want to make me feel better, we can test that theory. Tell your dad to trade Nolan Duggan."

Ellery laughs and I join her, and thank God that I have good friends, even if I can't have a good family.

## CHAPTER 8
# NOLAN

"What the actual fuck?" I growl and try not to choke. I wave a hand in front of my face aggressively, but it's useless. The smell won't go away or the glitter. The fucking glitter is everywhere.

The guys, of course, are no help. Every member of the team is laughing loudly and with abandon. Even Coach is snickering. "Okay, Duggan. I don't know who you pissed off, but there's no time to find out. Warm-up starts now."

"Is he shitting me? I can't hit the ice like this?" I am internally freaking. I got my second Secret Santa gift. It appeared on the bench in front of my locker while I was getting my skates sharpened. It was a small box and a card. I opened the box first and inside was a gaudy candle shaped like Santa Claus that reeked of pine. I hate the smell of pine. It makes me sneeze. Everyone knows this and makes fun of me because of it. After all, I'm supposed to be this burly mountain man from Alaska but the scent of a simple tree makes me sneeze uncontrollably.

I quickly moved away from the candle, leaving it in the box while I opened the card and - boom! It exploded in my face, glitter landing everywhere. And then it started playing "Jingle Bells."

"Holy shit. I can't believe she glitter-bombed you!" The Wall says as I keep trying to shake the red and green glitter off my face and jersey.

"Who? Who fucking did this?" I growl and Viktor just keeps laughing. "You said she."

"I didn't."

"You did. Jeremiah, you said *she* glitter bombed me," I repeat and step right up to him, grabbing his shoulder before he can fall into line with the rest of the team and trot out the door of the locker room. "Who is *she*?"

"I was speaking meteorologically," The Wall says quickly. He's finally stopped laughing. Now he just looks panicked.

"It's metaphorically, and no you aren't." I step closer to him.

He pulls his arm from my grip, claps me on the shoulder, and pushes me toward the door. "Let's go, Sparkles."

I get most of the glitter off before the actual game, but it doesn't stop the media from asking me about it in post-game interviews. Apparently the sparkle during warm-up was picked up on camera. Thankfully, we won solidly, and Viktor even got a shut-out, so the night wasn't a total fail. But I'm furious because after the game, I have to field questions about my agent's death and I'm pretty sure my heart-felt words lose a little impact because I look like a disco ball threw up on me.

"Nice goal there, Duggan," Xavier says. "Guess we should toss some glitter on you every game. Seems to have brought you some luck."

I flip him my middle finger. "That goal was for Rick. In his memory."

Coach walks in as we're all slowly pulling off equipment, basking in the glory of our win, and making fun of me, apparently. "Great way to go into the winter break!"

A few guys hoot, holler, and grunt their agreement. He informs us we have one more off-ice practice to do some weight training and review footage and plays the day after tomorrow, and then we're officially off for five days and back on the twenty-sixth for a practice before we board a plane for an away game on the twenty-seventh. "Don't forget we have the Christmas party Thursday evening," he explains. "Like last year, there'll be families from all over Vancouver here, and it'll be covered by the social media team. And…"

Coach says the word like a drum roll, and when I look up, the smirk on his face makes my blood run cold. "Felicity in Community Outreach has informed me that *Duggan* volunteered to play Santa for the kids this year."

Did I hear my name? Did he just say Duggan? I look up, and everyone is staring at me, most with complete and utter shock on their faces. "What?"

"Felicity said you're playing Santa this year," Coach repeats and he claps me on the shoulder. A piece of green glitter tumbles to the floor of the locker room. "I'm very happy to see you take a bigger part in community outreach, Duggan. I knew you could be a team player on and off the ice."

Well, now how can I refuse to do this? I can't. So instead, I want to swear. I want to scream. But most of all I want to find Felicity Roark and—

"Is this a trap?" Xavier asks after Coach leaves the room. "Like the real Grinch are you gonna throw on the Santa suit and steal from the kids or something?"

"You're right about one thing, it *is* a trap," I tell him. "But I'm the one caught in it, not the one laying it."

"You wish you were the one laying it…" The Wall snickers to himself and I lean forward to glare at him.

"So she's also my Secret Santa, isn't she?" I ask but don't

wait for a reply. "She glitter bombed me and now she's forcing me to be Santa Fucking Claus. Of course. It's all her."

"Umm...I'm pretty sure his middle name isn't Fucking," The Wall interjects.

"Yeah, I mean it's probably something less offensive, like Bob," Xavier replies.

"I bet it's Nicholas," Viktor suggests and they all nod.

"Yeah, totally. Good call Vik," The Wall says.

"Nicholas makes sense," Xavier agrees.

"None of this makes sense," I grumble as I head to the showers. "Least of all this asinine conversation."

The Wall starts signing "You're a Mean one, Mr. Grinch" as I walk away, so I biff the top of his head with the palm of my hand as I go.

# CHAPTER 9

# NOLAN

I'm out of the shower in record time, dressed back into my pre-game suit and storming down the hall with only one goal. Find Felicity Roark and make her pay for nominating me for Santa Claus. And I'm going to get her to confess she's my Secret Santa from hell too.

I find her in her office, packing up for the night. She's in cute little skirt and a tapered, girls-cut Comets shirt. She's also got a reindeer antler headband on. She's a fucking lunatic. I don't say a word, and even though her back is to the door as she packs her bag, she speaks. "What do you want Nolan? To wish me a happy holidays?"

"Fuck no," I reply. "I'm here to tell you to find someone else to play Santa. I am not your guy."

"But you *are* my guy," she says, turning to face me. Her bright blue eyes are dancing with amusement on the surface, but the longer I hold her gaze, the more I see the hard, defiant gleam at their core. "And I'm your girl, aren't I?'

For a second I vacillate on the double-entrendre in that statement. Why does she have to be as hot as she is frustrating? Truth is, from the moment I saw her, I was attracted to her.

Unfortunately, I met her within seconds of going on a two-month leave, so I didn't see her much. I wasn't at the rink while my knee healed except to sit in the team box to watch home games or attend some team meetings. But her pretty face and sweet smile had me thinking about her so much that I even went so far as to casually double check our policy about dating staff. But then Christmas happened and she came at it like a rabid elf, and that's a hard pass for me.

"I'm talking about Secret Santa," she clarifies before I can answer, yanking her purse up onto her shoulder and pulling her coat off the back of her chair. "You're mine aren't you?"

"I am not dressing up in a fat man suit to placate small children and be the laughing stock of this organization," I tell her, side-stepping her question.

She loses the amusement in her eyes now and crosses her arms over her chest. "You want to back out, then you tell Lance Isles yourself. He will be in tomorrow morning at eight. He was very happy that you were trying to take a proactive attempt to be involved with the community projects."

She starts to try and walk out right past me, but I grab her arm before she can slide out into the hall. She pivots fast, and we're face to face now. She's wearing heels that bring her closer to my height but not quite there, so I tilt my head down to make sure the fiery anger behind my eyes, isn't missed. "You already told Mr. Isles?"

"Yeah. Lance was thrilled," Felicity replies.

"Lance?" I cock my head. That just about confirms the rumors about how she got her job. No one calls the owner by his first name except his daughter's best friend, I guess.

"Mr. Isles," she corrects herself. "Now, let me go so I can go home and get back here refreshed and ready for whatever shitastic gift you'll be sending me next."

I smirk. It's a dead giveaway that I am, in fact, her Secret

Santa. It's fine. I'm done pretending. "Not a fan of that lovely yellow scarf you got today?"

"It's wool. I hate wool. It makes me itch just looking at it, and it's the color of cheap mustard," Felicity replies and shifts the subject again. "Lance...Mr. Isles and his daughter Ellery used to fund and operate a toy drive themselves ever since Ellery was six. He likes to spread joy, and when I started, he specifically asked me to heighten the team's community involvement at this time of year specifically. But feel free to tell him you aren't on board. Your contract is up next year right?"

That little reminder also makes me think of my recently deceased agent and the way I had to pay tribute to him in post-game interviews tonight covered in glitter. Thanks to this Christmas nightmare in front of me. She tries to leave again, but I'm not letting go of her arm. "Don't bring my contract into this, but if he doesn't re-sign me over this, so be it. I want my job because of how I perform not who I know."

Her big, ocean-colored eyes ice over. "Oh you're one of them? The people that think I was hired because Ellery made daddy do it," Felicity questions but continues before I can even nod. "For the record, I have a BA from Stanford in public relations and sports marketing and had a successful two-year stint for a major league baseball team before jumping to hockey. Ellery put my resume on top of the pile, sure, something Ellery's brother Deacon did for one of his frat brothers too when the position opened. But sure, let's just say that the female couldn't have possibly been hired on her work ethic, ideas and employment history. Misogynist."

She breaks free of my grip, because calling me a misogynist was like a blow directly to the solar plexus and weakened me. I stand dumb-founded for a second while she storms down the empty, darkened hall, past the elevators into a room at the end of the hall. I recover and follow after her. This is getting way more intense than I want it to be.

Yeah, I'm mad at her and she annoys me, but this is...too much.

It's a break room, apparently, I see as I reach the door and step into the rectangular space. Felicity is collecting a half-empty tray of Christmas cookies and putting them in a Tupperware to store overnight I'm guessing. They look like shortbread in the shape of snowmen and decorated with icing and colorful sprinkles. They're cute, even my dark heart has to admit that.

"I'm not a misogynist," I tell her, my voice probably softer than it's ever been with her, which causes her to pause. But she still won't look up at me. "I was raised by my two mothers in the wilds of Alaska, so let me tell you I've seen misogyny. I've seen what some of those mountain men have said to my mothers, and I'm horrified you'd think I was like them."

"Then don't assume that just because I know Ellery, I'm not qualified," Felicity says after a second and slowly lifts her gaze to meet mine across the table. She looks genuinely hurt, and my heart clogs with guilt. Fuck, I am an asshole. "Look at my work since I took over and tell me I haven't earned my position."

"I can't do that," I admit. "You're excellent at what you do. But do you have to go above and beyond for all this holiday crap?"

"What is your issue, once and for all?" Felicity says, leaving the Tupperware on the counter and placing her hands on her hips.

I run a hand through my still damp hair and sigh. "It's personal."

"Well, you're making it everyone's business, especially mine," Felicity replies and the fire in her words makes my dick twitch. She's super-hot when she's not perky and smiling.

"I'm not being Santa Fucking Claus." I growl and step around the table, into her space.

"Yes you fucking are!" She bellows back and steps into my space.

I'm tall, probably the tallest guy who's ever been in this break room, so maybe it didn't brush anyone else on the top of the head, but it skims my hair. I reach up and feel the leaves. I tilt my head, and there above me is the leafy green bundle of mistletoe. I tilt my head back down, and our eyes connect.

"Guess you're willing to ignore holiday traditions now that I'm the one under the mistletoe huh?" I'm honestly not sure why I say it. It comes out sounding like a taunt, like I'm daring her to kiss me. Am I? I don't know. All I can focus on is the tip of her tongue as it subtly skims her bottom lip before she bites it. She grabs the front of my suit jacket and yanks me forward. My hands instinctively grab her hips as our torsos collide, and she plants a kiss firmly on my lips. It's closed-mouthed. Hard, just a smashing of lips. But it's like Fourth of July fireworks going off in my chest, and my groin.

So when she starts to unclench her fists on my lapels, and the pressure of her mouth lightens, I press my fingers harder into her hips and hold her close to my body as I tilt my head and open my mouth, moving my tongue against her lips until she opens them. It's not a long wait. Her tongue rushes to meet mine, and then it's on.

Her hands tug at my suit jacket again, mine slide off her hips to her ass, cupping it roughly as I press my instant hard-on into her stomach. I push into her, she stumbles backwards, which is what I want, and as I bite her bottom lip, she lifts her left leg, and I move my hand to help her hook it onto my hip. She rocks her pelvis into me, her hands in my hair, nails scraping and creating a shiver that runs hot down my back. My lips move to her neck, just below her ear and I rasp out a threat.

"I wanna fuck you so hard those antlers fall off your pretty little head."

"I wanna suck your dick like it's a candy cane," she whispers back. "And I know you like how I suck candy canes."

Felicity Roark is pushing all my buttons, and this time, it's in the right way.

I lean in and capture her mouth with mine again. I rut myself up in the crook of her body, her skirt riding precariously high on her thigh as my hand slips across the smooth skin covered in sexy black stockings. They're thigh highs and when I get high enough I find bare flesh. We both shudder.

She pulls down my zipper on my dress pants and shoves her hand inside, pressing her palm into my underwear and against my thick length. Then she slips lower and cups my balls, and I bite her bottom lip. Her breath hitches as my exploring fingers find her underwear and then mine hitches when I find them damp.

PING.

Our eyes open and we tear ourselves apart with such force that her antler headband tumbles backward off her head. I catapult myself backward and hit a chair at the table with my hip, sending it tumbling to the tile floor with a clatter. Felicity turns her back on me and the door and immediately goes back to placing cookies in the Tupperware.

My eyes fly to the open door as I run my hands through my hair and I see Martine has stepped off the elevator and is looking at me quizzically. I feel caught even though I'd bet my contract she didn't actually see anything. She reaches the break room door and peeks in, finding Felicity and her cookies. Now she's holding the container and snapping the lid closed. "Hi you guys. Everything alright?"

"I'm going home," I bark and Martine scoots out of the way as I stalk out the door and over to the elevator. It's still there, so as soon as I punch the button, the doors open and I escape without another word.

The whole way home all I think about is that kiss and the wetness of the lacey fabric covering her pussy. Felicity is hiding some serious passion under that perky, proper, Type A exterior. She's not a delicate flower or a shy girl. She pressed herself into me and palmed my cock like she fucking owned it.

When I get home, Max is doing his ridiculous dead thing again, lying on his back with all his paws in the air on the end of the L-shaped couch. I take off my shoes and hang my jacket on the back of one of my dining room chairs. My hands run down the front of the lapels as I remember the way she yanked on them.

I throw myself down on the couch next to Max, who starts purring immediately. I give his belly an absentminded rub with one hand and undo my dress shirt buttons with the other. My brain is replaying every second of those moments in the break room on a loop. Max knows I'm distracted, so after thirty seconds, he swats at my hand, rolls over and trots off. "Sorry buddy," I whisper and start to undo my belt and dress pants. "But you probably don't wanna be here for this anyway. It would be awkward."

I slip my hand into my underwear and grip my hardened shaft, close my eyes and pretend it's Felicity.

# CHAPTER 10

# FELICITY

My face starts to flush as soon as I get out of my car and walk toward the arena. Oh my God, what the hell did I do last night? Making out with Nolan Duggan was inappropriate, out-of-character, the last thing I ever thought I would do and...felt incredible. The way he pawed at me, the way his tongue just decided it owned my mouth, the feel of his hands sliding up the inside of my thigh and his rock hard cock rubbing up against me.

"It's like the North Pole out here so why do you look like you have a sunburn?" Xavier asks me as he appears from the other side of what must be his Range Rover and falls into step beside me.

I stare at the pavement in front of my heels and try not to turn even more red. It's not really working. Ugh. "I'm just thinking about what a klutz I was falling over the other day."

I lift my still bandaged wrist. I'm supposed to go see the trainer today and he'll give it another once-over before I remove the tensor bandage completely. Xavier's dark blue eyes look skeptical. He lifts one of his thick, dark brows. "Funny, I thought maybe the flush was excitement at your next Secret

Santa gift you're giving. Maybe fill his locker with candy canes or cover him in tinsel this time?"

"I have no idea what you're talking about," I say calmly and pause as Xavier reaches for the door and holds it open for me.

"Look, I think the whole team has figured it out by now, probably even Nolan," Xavier replies and gives me a wink and a calming smile because I guess he can tell my blood pressure is spiking at being outed. "No one else gets under his skin as good as you do. Been that way since you started here, and we love it. But I gotta let you know, his issues aren't all invalid when it comes to avoiding the holidays."

"He won't get into specifics with me," I explain as we walk down the hall to the elevator. "And I know he's my secret Santa too, and he's doing his worst so it's only fair I do mine."

Xavier's eyes flare at that. "He's your Secret Santa?"

I nod and explain my oh-so crappy gifts so far. He's doubling over as we enter the elevator, and I have to hit the button for both of us. His laugh bounces off all the walls as the doors close and we descend. "Cucumber of the month? How did he know that was even a thing?"

"He's a smart cookie," I smile despite myself. Then I think of how his mouth felt all dominant and needy against my own and I start to flush again. Xavier, also a smart cookie, notices.

His smile turns heavier and more inquisitive. "This is more than just a Secret Santa Face-Off isn't it?"

"Of course not," I say airily. Too airily. My voice is too high and my shoulders shrug too quickly and now Xavier is really curious.

"Hmm..."

"Do not 'hmm' me!" I warn him, like I've got some moral high ground here, which I certainly do not. Nolan Duggan, the Comets Grinch, was seconds away from slipping his fingers into my panties last night, and I was disappointed when it didn't happen.

Xavier lifts his hands like I'm a cop with a gun. "Okay. Okay. But I really do believe that you two need to talk. Like, honestly and candidly about why you love Christmas so much and why he hates it, and I bet you'd both be glad you did it."

His rugged face grows serious, and he rests a friendly hand on my shoulder. "He's a really good guy. Honestly, I know people don't see that side of him much, but he is. Did you know he is fostering a kitten? He found it behind his apartment building, half frozen to death with a severe eye infection."

"What?" My hand raises to my chest and my mouth falls open. "Is it going to be okay?"

"Because of Nolan, yeah," Xavier nods. "He's paid for all its medical bills, he was waking up every four hours to feed it when it was really tiny, and he has a cat sitter that costs more than most babysitters when we're at away games. He swears he's not keeping it, just giving it a place to squat because the shelters are full. But I think he wants to keep it. He just isn't willing to admit it because then he's vulnerable. Nolan hates opening himself up."

I swear I let out an audible sigh. It's the kind of sigh a star struck fan lets out in the front row of a concert. Yeah, it's embarrassing and a dead giveaway that Xavier doesn't miss. His hand hits my shoulder again and he leans in close and smiles. "He's a good guy if you feel like calling a truce and giving him a chance."

The elevator lands on the ice level just as Xavier is finishing that sentence, and the doors open. Nolan is striding by, dressed in workout gear. He turns his head slightly to glance at whoever is in the elevator, but when he sees it's us, he stops dead in his tracks. He looks us both over, his amber colored eyes holding for a second longer than necessary on Xavier's hand on my shoulder. Something flickers across his features like he smelled something foul.

He's jealous? The thought sends a ripple of heat swirling through my belly. I don't like jealous men, but if Nolan doesn't like Xavier touching me it can only mean that he likes me, right? That thought is something that I shouldn't like, but I do. A lot. His eyes finally land on mine, briefly, but long enough that I feel another ripple of heat. Then Nolan looks at Xavier. "You're late."

"Don't you worry about me, Duggan," Xavier replies, and there's a slight taunting tone in his voice I don't like. He gives my shoulder a small squeeze before sauntering off toward the locker room. I step off too, and the elevator doors slide shut behind me. Nolan hasn't moved. He's in the hall, staring me down in a blue Comets tank top that puts his gloriously big arms on display. I've never seen a tattoo on him anywhere. He's one of the only guys that doesn't have visible ink. There's a rumor online with the puck bunnies that he has a hidden tattoo somewhere because no one can believe a tough, bold, grump like him could be ink-less. And of course a bunch of girls have volunteered to find out if he has one, by getting naked with him, but Martine quickly deletes those comments off our social media accounts. As we stare at each other now, I can't help but think that I would volunteer as tribute for that as well.

He steps forward, and I hold my breath.

"You looking to kiss Oakes under the mistletoe next?"

I blink. "What?"

"Maybe you should tie some up in the elevator and ride it up and down and you can kiss all of us eventually." Is he fucking serious right now?

"Stop being a jealous little bitch," I hiss under my breath so only he can hear. Our eyes connect, and I swear if someone else was in the hall right now, they would have grabbed the fire extinguisher against the wall. There have got to be visible sparks between us and not the good kind. These are all anger, no lust in sight. "If I wanted Xavier, I would have made a move by now. I've been here over a year and—brace yourself—not all men are repulsed by me. Now please don't talk to me again unless it's about the Santa outfit you're going to be wearing soon."

I storm off, shoulders back and trying to appear strong and brave, but really, I wish I could just cry. Does he really think I would flirt with Xavier? Less than twenty-four hours after I was groping and kissing him?

Luckily, Phil is waiting for me when I walk into his small therapy room so I don't have a chance to dwell on how shitty Nolan made me feel. "Let's take a look at that wrist, Felicity."

I smile and nod and push Nolan from my brain. When I get out of the trainer's room, the hallway is empty. It's also very quiet, and the door to the small conference room they use to review footage from previous games is closed. I assume the team is in there, so I take the opportunity to dart over to Nolan's locker. I dig my hand into my oversized purse to find his next Secret Santa gift. I bought it before the kiss, and I was warring with myself on whether or not to give it to him now. But that debate was settled when he reacted like a cave-man twenty minutes ago.

I place the gift on the little shelf above his warm up clothes and march back up to my office without looking back.

# CHAPTER 11
# NOLAN

Luckily, the guys had all left before I noticed the oblong thing wrapped in white paper peppered with cartoon Rudolphs. I pull it down from the cubby she placed it in and examine it. It's soft, like a towel or clothing except for the hard round thing wrapped separately and taped on top. I stare at it and think back to running into Felicity in the hallway earlier. If I really was Santa Claus, I would totally give myself a lump of coal for how I acted.

When those elevator doors opened and revealed her standing there huddled close to Xavier and he was touching her...something in me just snapped. I'd rather dress up as Santa Claus or get glitter thrown in my face every day for the rest of my life over seeing Felicity looking close and flirty with a teammate. I didn't realize that was the base root of what triggered me when I said all the stupidest things humanly possible to her, but it was. I enjoyed that kiss last night more than I've enjoyed anything in a long time, and deep down for me, it was a beginning to something more. Seeing her with someone else was a rude awakening that, number one, it might not happen again, and number two, she might not want it to.

Maybe the gift would give me a clear idea of what she is thinking. Did she enjoy our mistletoe moment as much as I did? Is she interested in me, in moving past our differences, like I suddenly am? I unwrap the larger, softer gift first. As the paper falls away I stare at what appears to be a black, rolled up piece of clothing. A T-shirt maybe? I unravel it and stare at it. I read the words printed across the chest of the shirt over and over.

*Duct Tape. It Can't Fix Stupid But It Can Muffle The Sound.*

I unwrap the round, hard thing even though I really don't have to. I know what it is. It is a roll of duct tape and there's a sticky note attached to it. The writing is clean, pretty cursive.

*Directions: Apply to your own face. Ho! Ho! Ho!*

"Ouch," I say to myself, and although it stings, hurts like hell, actually, I still smile. I decide right there that I can't give her the stupid gift I had already bought. It was a custom printed throw blanket with spiders all over it. They looked ridiculously realistic. Truth is I wasn't even sure Felicity hated spiders, I was just guessing. And now, even though her gift to me was a solid punch to my ego, I didn't want to swing back.

I had to do something else. Something that would really throw her off-balance. I had to play nice. I am staring off into space, trying to figure out how to do that, when Martine walks into the locker room. She sees me and stops dead. "Sorry. I thought all you guys went home. I wanted to get some footage of the room with the tree lit up for the 'gram."

I nod and stand up, grabbing my jacket and my stupid gift. I'm almost out the door when I stop. "Hey Martine? I need a favor."

She looks over at me and doesn't try to hide her shock. "Okay..."

I clear my throat. This is harder than I thought. "I'm Felicity's Secret Santa, and I've run out of gift ideas. Can you help?"

"You want me to tell you more about what she hates so you can torture her further?" Martine raises a dark eyebrow. "Not gonna do it."

"No. I want to know what she likes. So I can do something nice for once."

Martine raises the other eyebrow too now.

"I swear. Honestly."

She hesitates. I guess I must start to look as desperate as I feel, because after a minute, her face softens and she relents but not before threatening me. She points a finger in my direction. "Look, Nolan, if this bites me in the ass somehow, I will make your life hell. I have the power to make you look like an idiot with a tweet or an Instagram story. Remember that."

"Yeah. Yeah. If I'm lying, do your worst."

She inhales and then exhales slowly. "She has always wanted to go see the Aquarium Lights."

"What?"

"The Christmas lights display they do at the Aquarium," Martine explains. "It's amazing and a huge deal, but last year they were sold out every time she tried to reserve tickets. And this year, same issue. Oh and bonus points if it's this Friday because it's a Michael Bublé lights show, and all the lights are synchronized to his Christmas songs. He's her favorite."

"Oh." Of course little Miss Christmas wants to see Christmas lights and loves Michael Bublé.

"You know as well as I do that the hockey players in this town are local celebrities, and celebrities can get tickets to anything," Martine says.

I hate being that guy who uses my job as a way to get shit. I've refused free meals at multiple restaurants in this town. I don't take clothing or watches or anything unless they're a sponsor. I appreciate the gestures, but I already have so much, it seems greedy to take freebies. I rub my face as I ponder this. Martine is watching me with curious eyes. "Why the change of heart?"

I smile. "Because I realize I've been a little...harsh."

"Oh okay." I'm one foot into the hall when Martine stops me with her words. "Felicity is more than just not horrible. She's amazing at her job, and her positive attitude and ability to see the bright side has really improved the morale in corporate. She's the icing, makes everything sweeter."

I nod and am about to tell her that's a weird analogy when she grins. "And FYI, everyone knows you could use a little sugar to calm that vinegar side."

I roll my eyes, but as I pull out my phone to start pulling strings to get Felicity these tickets, I can't help but think Martine is right. I've tasted that sugar, and now I'm addicted.

# CHAPTER 12

# FELICITY

It's five minutes past five. I'm slowly putting on my coat in total disbelief. My eyes glued to the discarded wrapping paper in the trash can beside Martine's desk. Her Secret Santa got her the cutest set of Russian dolls. Every one was hand-painted to be a different *Schitt's Creek* character. A perfectly painted Johnny opened to reveal a perfectly painted Alexis which came apart to reveal an adorable Patrick, then David, then Stevie and finally the littlest one was Moira. Martine was obsessed with the show and squealed in excitement at the thoughtful gift.

I had gotten nothing today. Not a single stupid annoying thing. This was our last day in the office, except for the party tomorrow afternoon. So Nolan either forgot or wasn't playing anymore. And it fucking hurt. I was way more emotional than I should be about this but...I relied on these gifts to keep me perky. I didn't have anything else at Christmas. And even though this year Nolan decided to try and ruin it, I found myself looking forward to his horrible gifts too. Our fight was... fun. And that kiss... that was more than fun.

I take a deep breath as I head out for the night. It's shaky. I know I'm going to head straight home and have a big old pity party. There will be tears, and I'm not even sorry about it.

I don't know what I expected after that kiss but it wasn't this. Even after the blow-up this morning, I didn't think he would ghost me. I'm definitely happy I went through with giving him another mean gift. He deserves it. He's a Grinch inside and out, and I am better off without him.

I keep repeating that to myself, hoping my heart starts to listen so that maybe that dull ache in the center of it doesn't get any bigger, but then I step out into the staff parking lot. Nolan Duggan is leaning against the back bumper of my Kia Soul.

He's wearing an off-white cable knit sweater, his thick dark hair brushed back with a perfect little wave. His hands are stuffed into the pockets of his jeans, and his feet, crossed at the ankle, are covered in brown leather boots. He looks like heaven.

*But he's hell, Felicity. You know this!* My brain reprimands me.

He smiles. It's small and sheepish. I try not to smile back. I will not give in. "First things first. Sorry about earlier. I know I'm a crusty bastard, but that was extra, even for me."

I stop walking, my brain too shocked by that candid confession to make my feet move. He pushes himself off my car and up to his full six feet two inches of height. Man, does he look sexy as all hell in that sweater. But he's still a jerk. "Ok. Apology for that accepted, I guess. Have a good night, Nolan."

I try to walk by him to get to my driver's side door, but he steps in front of me so quickly I almost walk right into his chest. I look up, prepared to glare, but he's smiling again and man, it just steals my breath. "I am here to give you you're next Secret Santa gift."

Oh.

"But you have to come with me somewhere to get it."

*Oh.*

We stare at each other in complete silence. Two people from

sales wander by chatting as they head to their cars and don't even bother to look over at us. He shifts his weight a little. "Did that sound sketchy? Like serial killer sketchy or something? Because you're not saying anything. Nothing annoyingly perky or even sarcastic, and I'm kind of worried now."

Okay I can't not smile at that. "I know you're not dangerous. You're just a dick."

"Yeah, I got that message with your last gift," Nolan replies, and then he lifts his sweater with one hand, and I see he's wearing the shirt I bought him under it. I bite my cheek to keep from smiling. "Your gift is kind of time sensitive, so can you join me tonight?"

I swallow. "Okay."

He relaxes and motions with a tip of his head. "Let's take my ride. I promise I'll drop you back off here."

I nod because I don't know what else to do when you feel like you've fallen into the Twilight Zone. This whole thing feels off. But in a really good way. Like I won't be disappointed this time even though all this man has done is disappoint me. Well, and kiss me within an inch of my life and make my panties wet. But I digress...

We drive in silence, and it's not exactly comfortable, but it's not uncomfortable either. It's just odd, like everything else. I can't help but notice the cat carrier on the back seat and it reminds me of what Xavier said. "So you have a cat?"

We're at a red light, so he glances into the back seat and back to my face. He shakes his head. "Nope. I'm just watching a cat until someone adopts it."

"Fostering?"

"Yeah. Shelters were full when I found Max, but they said he'd likely be adopted by New Year's at the latest. People tend to adopt more around the holidays. They do it for their kids as presents or just cause they're lonely," he explains with a shrug that I can tell is meant to make me think he's non-committal. But is he?

"You named a cat you aren't keeping?" I question.

"Yeah. It was convenient to give him a name," he rationalizes. "But whoever adopts him can rename him. Max is chill. Totally easy-going. He won't mind."

Max. My brain makes a connection instantly, and I start to giggle. Nolan glances over at me again, quicker this time because he's moving through traffic. "What's so funny?"

"You named him Max?" I sputter. "And you're the Grinch."

"Yeah, the team and you call me the Grinch. So why does that make my cat's..." his voice trails off as he figures it out. He's smiling. It's occupying his whole handsome face, and then he bites back a laugh. "Shit. The dog's name in *How the Grinch Stole Christmas* is Max."

"Uh-huh," I wipe at the tears my giggles have brought. "You really didn't do that on purpose?"

"Hell no!" He laughs. "I do everything I can to fight that nickname."

"Except, you know, stop acting like a Grinch."

"Except that." He winks at me.

I grin. And then we enter the Stanley Park cosway and the sign for Aquarium pops up, and he turns. My mouth drops from a smile to a giant, gaping O. "Nolan...are you...did you manage to get me a ticket for the lights at the aquarium?"

That's not just a sweet, thoughtful gift, it's a sweet thoughtful gift that's spilling over with the one thing he loathes —holiday cheer. He looks like he might crawl out of his own skin, but he nods. "Yeah. I know you love this kind of thing."

"Oh my God! Oh my God! This is incredible!" I'm squealing with delight, and I may be humiliated about it later, but right now I just can't contain it. "I've been dying to go to this. You are...this is the sweetest thing ever."

"You might want to hold off on that praise because you have to go with me," Nolan says as he parks the car in their lot. "And I can't guarantee I won't scowl or roll my eyes. I know it's going to give me a migraine."

"I'll gleefully ignore you," I declare, and impulsively, I grab his hand as it leaves the steering wheel and squeeze it. "Thank you so much."

"You're welcome," he looks like he wants to say something else, but he doesn't. He just gets out of the car, and I jump out and almost sprint toward the gates, tugging him with me by his hand, which I've grabbed again.

Two hours later my heart is so full I think it might honestly burst. The lights Twinkling and blinking in time to Michael Bublé's Christmas tunes, while penguins and otters and polar bears swam in their pens and tanks is simply magical. And so is the chemistry between Nolan and me. We laugh together, we share poutine, and he mocks me for not putting condiments on the hot dog he bought me. I like them plain, sue me. And I mock him when he gets cotton candy, like a toddler. It's easy. It's fun. It feels just as right as it did when I was kissing him.

We come to the last row of displays way sooner than I would like, so I slow down and pretend to be enamored by the Christmas trees wrapped in rainbow lights and the eight-foot glowing Mr. and Mrs. Claus. He walks up and stands next to me, and without a word, takes his hand from his pocket and covers mine. His long fingers slip in-between mine, and I suddenly hate myself for wearing gloves. I want to feel our fingers tangled together.

"I hate Christmas because I've almost always spent it alone," he says quietly. "My moms live in Alaska. They own a construction business and run a lodge for my grandparents and never really get time off. They also don't have a lot of money."

I turn my head up to look at him, slowly, like moving quickly might scare him and stop this open door he's giving me into his life. He's not looking at me, he's staring straight ahead at the display. I gently squeeze his hand to show support but say nothing. He clears his throat and continues. "Alaska hockey leagues weren't my best shot at making the big time, so they used whatever spare money they had to get me into a fabulous private boarding school in Minnesota with an incredible hockey program. But we didn't have the money to fly me home on holidays. Any of them. So I spent it with whatever teammate's family took pity on me. It was always awkward, watching kids with their families, opening gifts that were picked by people who knew them so well and put so much thought into it while I opened boxes of chocolates or socks or whatever generic thing they'd wrapped so I wasn't empty-handed. And I was grateful for their kindness, but it was hard watching them hug their grandma and share inside jokes with cousins or whatever."

"I get that. I do," I say softly. Suddenly, all the pressure I put on him to just get into the spirit feels as mean-spirited as the joke gifts he sent me. "I'm sorry for giving you grief about it."

He finally pulls those golden eyes of his off the display and looks down at me, shaking his head. "No. Don't apologize. I need to get over it. Truth is, I have enough money to charter a plane now and go see my moms if I wanted to, even though we get less than a week off from hockey. Or I could fly them here, but...I don't know, it's almost like I refuse to let Christmas be good. It's like fuck that. I don't want to want it to be better."

I smile ironically. "I get that. I went in the opposite direction but for the same sort of reason."

His eyebrows raise. "Are you actually going to tell me why you're such a rabid little reindeer?"

I roll my eyes. "Yes. So shut up, walk with me, and listen."

He lets me tug him down the path, toward the exit. And I take a deep breath and continue to share my Christmas secret. "Two years ago, I was supposed to get married on December twenty-seventh."

I feel his step stutter a little, but I keep walking, eyes ahead like his were when he shared. "But on Christmas, I found out my fiancé was sleeping with another woman. He was my college sweetheart, and I even took the baseball job in Seattle to be close to him. He... worked in Washington State. Anyway, the other woman he cheated with, was my cousin."

"What a piece of shit."

Nolan's voice is thick with anger and the sexiest thing I've ever heard. I look up at him and the way his eyes are narrowed, and that very talented mouth of his set in a hard line is also making me wet. This is the best I've ever felt about what happened with Chet. "Oh and it gets better. You know how I found out? I woke up Christmas morning before everyone to make cinnamon rolls. My parents have a parrot. It's a heinous little bird that repeats whatever it hears. And it heard my cousin Jennifer and my fiancé, Chet, who snuck downstairs the night before when we were all supposed to be sleeping and were getting it on in the laundry room off the kitchen."

"Wh... what?" He sputters and he looks genuinely horrified, and a little bit stunned too. Because who wouldn't be when you find out a parrot blew up an engagement?

"Yep. I'm making cinnamon buns two days before my wedding, and Gonzo is squeaking 'oh Chet... that's it... oh. Promise me you'll leave her. Promise me. Oh Chet.'"

"HOLY SHIT." Is all Nolan can say. "Is he still with your cousin?"

"Yeah and my parents... well they kind of think that we all

just need to let it go for family's sake and other reasons," I mutter.

"Oh Felicity," he's switched from angry to sad, and I don't like it as much.

"Anyway, Ellery told me about the position with the Comets when she showed up for the wedding that wasn't going to happen. She was supposed to be my maid of honor. I didn't want to move home, and I was not going to go back to Washington with Chet." We reach the parking lot now, and his car is a few paces in front of us. "Anyway, I decided that Chet had ruined enough of my life. I wasn't going to let him ruin Christmas. So I've been on a mission to make every Christmas since a magical fucking wonderland of cheer and merriment."

He stops walking. I have to turn around and look up at him. He's staring at me like I'm insane, and honestly, maybe I am. But then after blinking a couple times, he breaks into another one of those big, bold, beautiful smiles I didn't think he was capable of just one week ago. "I'll never bug you about being a rabid little reindeer again. I promise."

I'm pressed up against him now, chest-to-chest, and he cups the back of my head and claims my mouth in a kiss that blows the doors right off our last kiss. Because this one is fueled by a fire stronger than anger. The fires of truth. We stand there in the parking lot, Christmas lights twinkling all around us, making out like hot and heavy teenagers for a very long time. It's me who breaks the kiss first. "Can we go somewhere private so we can do things to each other that will put us on Santa's naughty list?"

"I thought you'd never ask."

# CHAPTER 13

# NOLAN

Somehow, even though it feels like all the blood in my body is now living in my throbbing cock, I manage to drive us safely back to my place. As soon as I'm parked, I can't keep my hands off her. Luckily, she doesn't seem to mind, and we grope each other and make-out all the way to the elevator and all the way up to my penthouse. As soon as we step inside, I have her jacket off and am trying not to just rip the buttons off her top.

Her hands are undoing my belt and jeans. Her mouth is on my neck, lips and tongue sucking and sliding along the side, making my balls tighten and tingle. And then she speaks words so fucking hot my mind melts. "Every time I see you in the locker room, I have the urge to lift my skirt, climb into your lap, and fuck that gloomy look off your fabulous face, and I hate myself for it."

I have enough of her blouse undone now that I can yank her bra down a little bit and cup her breasts. "Every time you smile or bellow out a cheery good morning, I want to haul you into a dark corner of the building and do this."

I dip my head down and suck on her left breast. She shudders and lets out a breathy expletive. I bite her nipple and she gasps. Her hand cups my cock and squeezes. I grunt and wrench my mouth from her tits and take her mouth in another hard and dirty kiss.

There's a meow from my living room. She breaks away from my mouth to tilt her head and find the source. I growl and glare over my shoulder at Max who is in his usual spot on the sofa. "Max meet Felicity."

"Hi Max!" She waves at him, and his tail does a swirl like he's waving back. "Oh my god, Nolan he's beautiful."

"Not as beautiful as you are naked, I'm sure."

She blushes, and I finish undoing her blouse. My lips kiss the shell of her ear, and then I push her blouse to the ground and pull her down the hall to my bedroom, watching her beautiful breasts bounce as we go.

Five minutes later, we're skin-to-skin and all the playful kidding is over. We're needy in a serious way, grabbing and rubbing and kissing and panting. I reach for the drawer in my nightstand and pull out a condom, but I drop it on the bed and lie down on my back between the condom and Felicity. She rolls towards me curling her naked body against the side of mine and holds my cheek in her palm as her tongue slides into my mouth and across mine. When the kiss breaks, my voice is so husky with arousal I don't recognize it, but the words are all me. "I want you to reach up and grab that leather headboard with both hands and then straddle my face so I can lick you until you come all over me."

She lets out one of those breathy little gasps again. But she grants me my wish and as her pretty little pussy hovers half an inch from my face I whisper "It's a fucking Christmas miracle" before I take my first lick.

She lets out a throaty moan, and my restraint rides away on it. I lick her with abandon. She moans louder the wetter she gets, and then, when I add some fingers to the mix, she arches her back, and the only sound she makes is desperate panting. Her hips gyrate, helping me with a needy rhythm, and when my lips find her clit and I flick my tongue over it again and again, she breaks, coming hard across my fingers and mouth.

It may be selfish, but I barely give her a chance to ride it out before I reach up and pull her by her hips, guiding her off of my face and onto her back. The only care I show is to the condom as I roll it on carefully so it doesn't tear and then I align myself with her entrance and push her hair off her face. Her eyes flutter. "Don't hold back now."

So I don't. I slide right into her hard and fast, and holy shit I see stars. Or Christmas lights. Something sparkly and absolutely magical. I pump into her over and over at a relentless pace and she grabs my ass and holds on, not letting me slow down. Not that I want to. But then, I feel her tighten and she looks me right in my eyes, which I'm sure are crazed with lust and she says. "You make me so fucking wet at work I've thought about masturbating to you on my lunch break."

"Oh fuck." I completely lose control and explode inside of her like one of those canons they use to hurl T-shirts into the stand at games.

I collapse on top of her, and she wraps her arms lazily across my shoulders, sighing contently. I focus on the pounding of her heart against mine. They're oddly in sync, just like we are now. "Felicity?"

"Yeah?"

"This is the best holiday memory I've made."

"Play your cards right, and I'll make your New Year's pretty memorable too," she quips.

"I'm gonna hold you too that," I whisper back. "And please pencil me in for Valentine's Day, Easter and President's Day too."

She lets out a breathy giggle, so I feel the need to add. "I'm not kidding, Felicity. You and me, this is a thing. I don't want to stop."

Her laughter fades and she tilts her head so we can look at each other. A gentle blush creeps back into her cheeks. "I was hoping you'd say that."

I kiss her. A soft promise of all that's still to come.

"Nolan?'

"Yeah?"

"You still have to dress up as Santa tomorrow."

"Argh!" I growl but I'm smiling into her neck.

Because she won. This woman won the stupid little competition we were having, and my heart. I'll do anything for her. Just like the damn cat, she's here to stay. And just like with Max, I'm not the least bit upset about it.

## CHAPTER 14
# FELICLITY

"You're smiling pretty big," Ellery notes as she breezes into my office. She's wearing a full-length, faux fur coat in a glittering, pristine white, and her arms are piled with bags. She plops them all on my desk, covering the entire surface. "That must mean everything is going smoothly for the party?"

"Actually, the pouring rain means we have to move the party inside and no one is ready for that, the inflatable reindeer has a whole in it, and Santa's throne is still being constructed because they lost the screws that hold it together and had to run to the hardware store, " I inform her as I stand up, because I can't see her through the mountain of gifts she dropped on my desk. "And apparently, we still have wrapping to do."

"Never fear, I wrap at the speed of light," Ellery shrugs out of her coat. "If everything is chaos, why are you smiling then?"

I stare at her and bite my lip. Then I shift my eyes to the hallway through my open door. I don't see anyone out there, so maybe I can tell Ellery and no one will overhear. I step around my desk, close my door and lean against it. "Because I had sex. And it was ah-mazing."

Ellery squeals and I shush her, so she covers her mouth and jumps up and down, her hair bouncing off her shoulders. "Who? How? When?"

"The when, last night. The how, missionary, then a little reverse cowboy this morning," I blurt out and she starts jumping again. "And the who... Nolan Duggan."

Ellery squeals again and I shush her, but she isn't listening. She rushed to me and grabs me by the shoulder. "You made the Grinch's heart grow two sizes!"

"Well something grew two sizes, that's for sure," I laugh and she hugs me.

"Wait is this... like more than a one and done holiday hook-up?" Ellery questions.

I give her a small shrug. "It's more. I mean, for me. And for him, I think. His post-orgasm talk was all promises. But I'm still a little nervous."

"I hope it is," Ellery announces and smiles at me tenderly. "I know he's gruff, but he's a good guy. And you deserve a good guy, Felicity."

"Thank you," I smile. "I think you're right. On both counts. We have plans to meet up after the party, so we'll talk more then."

She hugs me again. "I want text updates tonight. Before more banging. Or after. Whatever works, but keep me updated."

I laugh. "Okay, but for now, let's concentrate on getting everything right for this event. I want to be able to watch Nolan play Santa without putting out fires."

"Ha! This really must be serious if he hasn't backed out," Ellery quips, and we both walk over to my desk to wrap the extra gifts she brought for the kids who are attending.

～

Two and a half hours later, the amazing crew at the arena have solved all my problems. They decided to cover the ice with the floors they put down for concerts and bring the food trucks in through the Zamboni entrance. We've set up Santa's throne at one end and the crafts and games tables at the other. The inflatable reindeer and snowmen are peppered throughout. The place is packed with families and kids, and everyone looks like they're having a good time.

"Nice job, Roarke," Jeremiah says as he walks over to me, a giant paper cone of truffles fries in his hand.

"Thanks," I say proudly and steal one of his fries. "I think Mr. Isles is pleased with the result."

I look over to where he's standing by a six-foot inflatable snowman with some other men in suits, who are likely either investors or local advertisers. Both were invited. I look at up at Jeremiah as I chomp on my stolen fry, and he winks at me. "I was talking about your work with the Grinch. He's been de-grinched. Walked into the locker room smiling and is happily putting on his Santa outfit as we speak."

"Happily?"

"Well he's not swearing," Jeremiah explains, and I laugh. He nudges my shoulder with his own. It's kind of like being hit with a bowling ball. Jeremiah is a tank. "I'm guessing you two decided to play nice?"

"Very nice," I admit and try to tone down my grin.

He chuckles knowingly, but it's interrupted by Martine, who runs over to grab my arm. "You need to announce Santa. He's ready and almost as uncomfortable as a dog in a Christmas sweater. So do it now before he changes his mind."

She starts pulling me across the cavernous space, darting in between people until we reach the microphone next to Santa's throne. She shoves it at me and pulls her phone out of her back pocket to film. "Your panties are going to legit drop when you see him, Felicity. His shoulders and biceps are bulging out of the costume, and he refuses to wear the big cotton belly so he kind of looks like a Chippendale Santa. The moms will definitely appreciate it."

I want to go back there and make him wear the stuffing, but I don't have time as Martine says. "Go! I'm gonna hit record on Instagram."

I blink and clear my throat and turn on the microphone. "Hey kids! Santa is here! Come line up to get your picture taken on his jolly, little lap!"

There's a flurry of activity around me as all the kids scramble away from whatever they were doing to make their way towards me. And then Nolan saunters out looking like a pornstar Santa. Oh my God he is HOT. My jaw literally drops, and Ellery, who has walked up beside me, has to shove me to get me to close my mouth. He didn't just skip the belly. He skipped the silly white cotton beard as well and opted to use white and silver temporary spray to coat his own beard and dark hair. It's more of a silvery salt-n-pepper than a white, but nobody seems to care. Martine is right, all the mothers are eyeing him like he's candy. I can't blame them.

"You owe me for this," he whispers as he passes me. "But don't worry, you'll enjoy the repayment too."

I flush from the tips of my toes to the top of my head where my antler headband is. Ellery lets out a small whistle. "You make sure to spank this naughty girl later, Santa."

Nolan blinks and I shush her. "Children!"

She giggles and steps away to help organize the chaos that is the children trying to line up. I watch for what has to be a full hour as Nolan gently lifts kid after kid onto his lap and listens patiently as they talk to him. He nods and even smiles – repeatedly. And then they move on to Jeremiah and Xavier, who give each child a wrapped present as they leave.

He looks at me sometimes between kids and winks or smiles. God, I am falling fast for this man. So very, very fast. The last kid climbs up on Nolan's lap as Mr. Isles waves me over to where he's standing a few feet away.

"You really are a miracle-worker Felicity," Mr. Isles says as I come to a stop beside him He's smiling at me with pride. "I really can't thank you enough for how well you run these events. They mean as much to me as the games, really."

"It's not just me, sir, but thank you," I say humbly and return his smile. "I'll make sure the team knows how happy you are."

"I was just telling your dad what an incredible job you do," Mr. Isles continues, and I feel my shoulders tense. It's not uncommon for a team owner to talk to a sports agent, except last time I checked, my dad didn't rep anyone on the team. Which is another reason why I decided to take the job. My dad's client list is mostly baseball, and I wanted to steer clear of him as much as Chet.

"I didn't know you knew my dad," I reply, hoping I don't sound too cold. Mr. Isles doesn't need or deserve my attitude.

"I didn't until today." Mr. Isles says. "He's here as Nolan's guest. I thought you knew."

"I... I'm... no. I didn't know," I sputter because his words are floating around my brain like pieces of a jigsaw puzzle that don't seem to fit together. "Nolan? Duggan? Invited my dad here?"

"Yes," Mr. Isles says, and his salt-n-pepper eyebrows furrow. Then his dark eyes move past me and he waves at someone else. "Harvey! You didn't tell your daughter you were coming?"

"Wanted to surprise her," Dad's voice hits my ears, and I turn as see him walking toward me. He's in a suit. And behind him, done with playing Santa but still in the outfit, is Nolan.

His eyes are as wide and shocked as mine. I have no idea what's going on, but I'm not liking it at all.

"Surprise honey! When your mom found out I was coming here to sign Nolan, she filled the trunk with gifts for you."

"Sign Nolan?" I swallow. "You're going to rep Nolan?"

My eyes land on Nolan. He averts his stare. "Mr. Roarke can we talk about this later? This is an event for the kids and I—"

"Of course. Of course. Go be merry and bright," Dad tells Nolan.

"Felicity..." Nolan says my name and steps towards me, but I step away.

I plaster the biggest smile I can on my face and announce, "I'm going to see how our VIP guests are doing in the suite upstairs."

"I should go with you," Nolan says. "That's where the kids with mobility issues are right? They should have their time with Santa too."

"Great idea!" I say, and my voice is a little too shrill to be considered cheery, but I hope no one takes note. "You go do that. I'm going to help Ellery at the games table."

"But —"

"You're on your own," I say tersely and storm away as fast as I can.

# CHAPTER 15

# NOLAN

She disappears into the crowd before I can sputter out a complete sentence. Left in her wake is this undeniable cloud of awkwardness. I turn and see Harvey Roarke and Mr. Isles staring at me, confused.

"I'm heading up to the suite to see those kids," I mutter and start to walk away.

"I'll walk with you," Harvey tells me and falls in step beside me.

We walk in silence all the way off the ice, down the tunnel and to the elevator that will bring us up to suite level. It isn't until we step inside and I punch the button that I speak. Still staring straight ahead I say. "Felicity is your daughter?"

"Yeah. My one and only," Harvey says. "Unless you don't like her and then, never seen her before in my life."

He laughs. It's not a funny joke.

"I like her. A lot," I reply, finally turning to look at him. "Which is why I'm concerned you told her I invited you here. I didn't."

"Well, you invited Rick," Harvey explains. "I work for the same agency as him. Well that he used to work at. I normally rep baseball players but I'm branching out, and so when I saw the invite on his desk as we were clearing it out with his widow, I decided to come. Introduce myself. You're going to need someone to rep you, and I'm more than happy to be that person."

I grunt out a sound, like a "Huh" but much meaner sounding. Harvey's smile dims. He shoves his hands in the pocket of his designer suit. "So you like Felicity?"

"She's wonderful," I tell him and take a low slow breath. "I think... well, I think we have something special, her and I. We kind of just started dating."

His eyes widen so much it smoothes the crinkles by the corner of his eyes, and then his smile is back full force. It's similar to his daughter's — wide and bright — but not as warm. "Amazing! Great news! Another reason to sign with me. Keep it in the family."

The elevator doors slide open and we're high above the ice now, on the floor that has a string of V.I.P suites. The doors are open to one at the end of the hall, and I hear happy chatter. Harvey steps out with me. "You know I rep her ex. Felicity used to date a baseball player."

"Yeah, she mentioned it," I bark and then pause, my eyes narrowing on him. "You used to rep her boyfriend? The dude who cheated on her when they were engaged? Days before the wedding?"

Harvey looks shocked I know that much. "Umm.. yeah. I think the cheating... well, we all make mistakes. Chet and Jennie are just a better fit than Chet and Felicity. And he feels really bad. He paid us back for all the deposits on the venue and the food."

"And you dumped him right?" I prod and cross my arms over my chest. "You don't still rep the man who screwed your daughter over?"

"I do," Harvey admits, and he doesn't even look like he feels the least bit bad about it. "I keep my business and private life very distinct. So if things didn't work out with you and Felicity, you don't have to worry about that affecting our business relationship."

This guy... man. I can't believe he doesn't get it. But he doesn't. And poor Felicity has probably got relationship PTSD thinking I would sign with her dad. I uncross my arms and extend my hand. He shakes it, thinking it's some sort of deal, but it's a kiss-off.

"Well that's not the type of man I want to do business with, Harvey," I say flatly. "No offense, but your daughter is incredible and sweet and kind, and I'm picking her even if you aren't. Sorry you wasted a trip out here. Have a nice flight home."

I turn and start to walk away but pause and turn back to him. "Oh and merry Christmas."

"Uhhh... merry Christmas?" he sputters completely shell-shocked.

"Mine will be great," I call back. "Spending it with Felicity and my cat."

I leave him in the hall and step into the room filled with more kids. All I want to do is find Felicity, but this is important to her, so I'll stay put and be the best damn Santa she could ask for. Then I'll find her and convince her I can be the best damn boyfriend too.

# CHAPTER 16

# FELICITY

The arena is entirely quiet now. The lights on the ice are off. The families, vendors and staff have all vacated the premises, and I'm betting most of the players have too. I'm doing one last sweep of the Community Suite to make sure none of the guests left anything behind.

The suite door opens, and I expect to see a member of our cleaning team. They would be a few hours early, but no one else should be up here now. So when I see Nolan Duggan filling the entire doorway with his hulking frame, still wrapped in his Santa suit, I'm shocked. What doesn't shock me is the scowl on his handsome face.

"Can I help you?" I ask airily. I'm beat — dog tired — after working all day, but I am exerting every last bit of energy to seem overly perky and bright just to annoy him. His frustration gives me strength.

"You think I would invite your father here and not tell you?" he growls.

"I don't know what to think," I correct him. "But I know that he was here. And he's an agent. And a very quick Google search showed me you're currently agent-less."

"Yeah and your dad is apparently an agent with the same company that my agent worked at before he passed away. Something you left out the other night. That he's an agent. An agent that reps your cheating ex. Chet is it?" he growls, stepping further into the suite, the door closing behind him. He looks so incredibly intense, and if I didn't know better, I'd find him intimidating, but something I know now: Nolan Duggan is like the Doberman my grand dad had on his farm in Upstate New York, all bark and no bite.

So I walk right up to him to stand less than a foot away, shoulders back and head tipped up because he's tall. Six foot something. I'm only five foot eight in my heels. "Well excuse me for not sharing the most humiliating part of my backstory with you the first chance I got. I thought that part could be shared later. I thought we had time to get to know all each other's dirty little secrets. I guess I was wrong."

"Why do you guess that?" He's growling again, and I hate that my panties are getting wet from it.

"Because I don't date men my father reps. It's proven to be way too messy."

"And you want to date me?"

"Nolan."

He steps right up to me, so close we bump. But I'm feeling vulnerable and confused, and so I step back and fold my arms over my chest, covering my nipples which have decided to stand at attention and join the raging party that was being thrown by my hormones. "I don't normally do one night stands. And I know we didn't exactly talk about what last night was, but I was... I mean. Oh forget it. Sign with my dad. He's a great agent. Let's forget this ever happened."

He stares so intensely at me that it only serves to heat my insides up even further. Now I can feel my cheeks pinking. Why does he have to look so damn fine as a furious Santa Clause? He turns those amber and brown eyes on me. They're fringed with the darkest lashes I have ever seen. I couldn't achieve that level of lushness even with all the mascara on the planet. "You give up really easily don't you?"

"I fight when it's right."

"And you don't think we're right?" he grumbles. His eyes aren't on my face. They're bobbing between the room and... my middle? Or my.... Chest? Is he watching my chest?

I don't want to look down, but I shift a little. The fabric of my blouse rubs against my body. My buttons feel like they haven't popped. Man, why didn't I wear a padded bra? I can feel the fabric graze against my already turned-on nipples. Oh fuck.... Is he...?

Suddenly, he reaches out and puts a warm hand on each of my forearms, rubbing them gently. He's smiling down at me with this grin that is dark but not deadly like the smile he usually sports in my presence, if he sports one at all. This smile is... feral. In a delicious way.

"Wh... why are you doing that?" I sputter softly, my voice somehow incapable of anything higher than a stage whisper in this moment. It's his scent... the remnants of after shave — warm, sensual with tones of cinnamon and cloves — on his jacket and the heat of his broad chest just inches from my nose.

"You're cold." Nolan declares it. It's not a question.

"No. I'm not," I argue. "The suites are heated."

How can he not feel that? It's perfectly comfortable in here, externally. And internally well, I'm far from chilly. I'm just about ready to combust. But he doesn't need to know that. And then our eyes meet and that delicious smile deepens, and those eyes with their big flecks of amber slip lower again, and I realize... he knows. His tongue slips out and slides slowly across his bottom lip. "If you're not cold, then you're turned on. Nipples, like hips, don't lie, Felicity."

"Oh my God," I hiss softly as my cheeks turn from pink to fire engine red and I quickly fold my arms across my chest again. "This is highly inappropriate!"

"Not if you're my girlfriend," He replies, and when I move to step around him, he moves with me so we're toe-to-toe and his big, broad chest is in front of nose still. Oh fuck, I have to get away from him. "So why don't you stop arguing with Santa and admit we're right for each other? You're just scared."

"I don't date men who work with my father," I manage to repeat. My heart is beating at double-time.

"I'm not working with your father," Nolan replies and even dares to shrug at me. "I picked you Felicity. Just like he should have."

And just like that, my vision blurs with tears. I wasn't expecting them, and neither was he. I try to blink them back as he panics. "Hey! No one cries in front of Santa."

"Lots of kids do!"

"But you're not a kid! Stop," he begs. "Crying women freak me out."

I manage to keep the tears from falling and choke out a little laugh. The tension on his handsome face eases, and he steps towards me again. "Now admit it, you think we're right for each other."

"I think... we're so wrong we're right," I admit with a shy smile.

"Yeah. I think that pretty much sums it up," He grins at me and lifts a hand to run it through my hair, which I left loose today. "So... now what?"

"Now we go home so I can sit on Santa's lap," I reply with a flirty smile.

"Or how about..." He grins back at me. It's feral again. And this time I don't fight the flush it brings. He reaches up and gently plucks my antlers off my head. "How about we stay right here and you sit on Santa's face instead?'

I am frozen, but not in fear... in embarrassment? No. In *desire*. Desire has me rooted to the floor of this suite, unable to move away from him. All I can see is the rough stubble on his dimpled chin, covered in that temporary silver-white spray dye and the glint of lust in his hazel eyes and the scent... that woodsy scent of his that makes me feel as primal as he looks.

"Nolan... you're naughty," I whisper. He's right up against me, my hard nipples rubbing up against his chest through the flimsy fabric of my blouse, sending shivers of lust down my spine. I need to start wearing sweaters to work if I'm going to be this turned on by him from now on. Thick, impenetrable sweaters.

"I said I would play Santa, but I didn't say I would be PG." He smiles, slowly. And then I feel his thumb under my chin, and he starts to tilt my head up so our eyes lock. And I let him because the feel of his rough fingers under my chin is excruciatingly sexy.

"Nolan Duggan," I repeat his name in a strong whisper because that's all I can manage with the tingle shooting down my spine as his fingers ghost my neck. "You are a stubborn, grumpy, gruff, royal pain in my ass."

"Uh-huh." His smile is simply too much to handle. I can't bear it. I have to get it off his face. "I'm also your boyfriend."

I grab his face in my hands, barely registering the rough brush of his stubble on my palms before I pull him down and our lips connect.

It's instant fireworks inside me, everywhere. Sparks and heat and brilliant bright desire course through me. His big hands grab my waist and yank me closer. I knew he would be rough and demanding, like last night. Like the kiss in the staff kitchen. And my girl bits are jumping for joy. Because he's all mine now and not going anywhere.

I don't have to deepen the kiss, he does it for me. His tongue demanding entrance and then sweeping over mine with a rough dominant pass. Before I realize it's happening, I'm moving backward. Nolan is guiding me to the large couch at the back of the suite, near the small kitchenette area where the catered food goes. I reach up and hold onto his tie, pulling him down with me when he pushes me over the low arm of the couch and onto my back across it.

He breaks the kiss long enough to smile down at me. "Tell Santa what you want for Christmas?"

"For you to find something else to do with your mouth besides talk."

I lean forward trying to kiss him again, but he pulls away with other ideas, clearly. His lips find my neck, and my eyes flutter closed. One of his hands snakes up under my skirt and makes it all the way to my hip bone before I open my eyes again. "Nolan..."

"I'm going to do something other than talk with my mouth," he tells me. "Unless you tell me rabid little Christmas elves like yourself have something against getting their pussy licked."

Holy shit. Is this real life? Am I actually going to let him do this right here and now? Of course I am.

And then he drops to his knees, and his lips start a path from my knee upward, his hands pushing my skirt up higher and higher to clear the way. By the time he gets to the highest point of my inner thigh, I'm panting in anticipation. When his tongue slides delicately across my folds, I moan. He smiles. I can feel it by the scrape of his beard against my inner thighs. I fucking hate that my weakness for him is bringing him satisfaction. So I slip my fingers through his dark, thick hair, which is still damp from his post-game shower, and I force out an ulti-matum in order to pretend I have control over the situation at all.

Nolan has got mad skills with a stick on the ice and with his tongue off the ice. I'm writhing and quivering within seconds. I want to fight it though, to make him work, and I know he wants to work. Our push-and-pull, tug-o-war relationship isn't changing just because it's official. He slides two fingers into me at once and his lips find my clit, his tongue lapping it eagerly. "Fuck, Felicity, you are too stubborn to come? Really?"

"Maybe you're... just... not... oh my god..." I bite back another moan. "Good enough."

"Shut up little Christmas elf, and come on Santa's tongue already," he whispers back.

And damn... I do. I come like I'm free falling off a cliff. Every-thing gets hot and light, my legs, my arms my belly... I'm floating and burning in the most delicious way. My fingers curl into his dark hair and hold on like if I let go, I'll be lost forever.

Finally, after what feels like a century, my soul finds my body again. Nolan pulls away slowly, and I come crashing back to reality. I just let my arch nemesis between my legs. And I liked it. More than words can say. Not that I would ever admit it, especially because he's staring at me with such an arrogant smile right now. And he's got my lace panties swinging from his index finger. I scramble to a standing position and reach for them but he holds them up above his head. And even in heels, I can't reach them.

"Nolan," I scold and smooth my hair, which must be all over the place. "Those are mine."

"I think I'm keeping them," he replies smugly. "As a trophy."

"You can't!" I bark, but he just keeps on smiling that punch-able, and okay a little bit fuckable, smile. I sigh. "Fine. Keep them."

I head to the door, and I kind of want to high-five myself for not walking like a newborn fawn. My legs feel so wobbly after that epic orgasm that I wouldn't have been surprised if they gave out. But I manage to make it all the way to the door to the suite in a few confident strides. I fling it open. The air that wafts in flies right up my skirt, making me intimately aware of how bare I am down there. "You can keep them for now, but I'm going to win them back."

"How?" He asks as we walk down the hall and he slings a lazy, possessive arm over my shoulders.

"Because when we get home, I'm going to finally suck you like I was sucking that candy cane last year."

His step falters, and I giggle and keep walking.

"We might not make it home," he warns and regains his stride, chasing after me and grabbing me around the waist and kissing my neck softly as we wait for the elevator.

Who would have thought I'd fall for the Grinch at Christmas? But damn did I fall, *hard*. And best of all, he fell for me too.

# Acknowledgments

Thank you to author Sierra Hill for including me in Scoring Over The Holidays, which was the original reason I wrote this novella. And lots of love to the other authors involved who made my first anthology experience a ton of fun.

Thanks to my husband Jack, my fur ball Gus, and my mom for always making sure my holiday season is a fun one. Thanks to my agent Kimberly Brower and her team at Brower Literary. Thanks to my editor Katie Kenyhercz, my beta and bestie Sarah Jillain, and the amazing Jillian at Blue Moon Creative Studio for the pretty cover.

Thank you to the readers for picking up this quirky little novella. I hope Felicity and Nolan brought you some holiday cheer. I'm going to make the Comets an annual holiday novella series. In 2023 you'll get Jeremiah 'The Wall' Waller's story. In the meantime, have a holly, jolly 2022 Christmas!

# About the Author

Victoria is a Canadian and former Californian who currently lives in a 222 year-old house with her husband, their grumpy Chihuahua, Gus, and more spiders than she cares to think about. She's a firm believer in happily ever after - in books and in real life.

For more books by Victoria Denault, head to victoriadenault.com